"SOMETIMES," GRACIE SAID, "I JUST WANT TO forget about the things I have to do, the things I see, but . . . I can't."

Max wanted to make her feel better. Wanted to offer comfort, sympathy, but he didn't know how. Forgetting, though—he was good at that. His gaze dropped to her mouth, to her tempting lips, trembling in invitation. "If forgetting is what you're after," he said, lowering his voice, "I think I can help you out."

Her gaze widened, linked with his. A pulse beat at the hollow of her throat where her khaki shirt was unbuttoned. "How?" It came out a whisper.

Smiling, he watched her moisten her lips as her breath came faster. He cupped her chin, slid his hand down the smooth skin of her neck and up again. A kiss or two, nothing more, he thought. He tilted her head back and bent his own to taste her. Sweet. Salty. Sexy. His tongue traced the seam of her lips until they parted. She accepted his tongue, drawing it in and meeting it with darting thrusts of her own.

Indulging them both, he put his arms around her, pulled her closer, and took the kiss another level deeper.

WHAT ARE *LOVESWEPT* ROMANCES?

They are stories of true romance and touching emotion. We believe those two very important ingredients are constants in our highly sensual and very believable stories in the LOVE-SWEPT line. Our goal is to give you, the reader, stories of consistently high quality that may sometimes make you laugh, sometimes make you cry, but are always fresh and creative and contain many delightful surprises within their pages.

Most romance fans read an enormous number of books. Those they truly love, they keep. Others may be traded with friends and soon forgotten. We hope that each LOVESWEPT romance will be a treasure—a "keeper." We will always try to publish

LOVE STORIES YOU'LL NEVER FORGET
BY AUTHORS YOU'LL ALWAYS REMEMBER

The Editors

Loveswept® 877

AMAZING GRACE

EVE GADDY

BANTAM BOOKS
NEW YORK · TORONTO · LONDON · SYDNEY · AUCKLAND

AMAZING GRACE

A Bantam Book / February 1998

ISBN 0-553-44630-4

Published simultaneously in the United States and Canada

Bantam Books are published by Bantam Books, a division of Bantam Dou-
bleday Dell Publishing Group, Inc. Its trademark, consisting of the words
"Bantam Books" and the portrayal of a rooster, is Registered in U.S.
Patent and Trademark Office and in other countries. Marca Registrada.
Bantam Books, 1540 Broadway, New York, New York 10036.

PRINTED IN THE UNITED STATES OF AMERICA

OPM   10 9 8 7 6 5 4 3 2 1

For Mom and Dad with love

ONE

Some days it just wasn't worth getting out of bed.

Hell, Texas. Population 892, if you counted cows and chickens. Since it was hardly big enough to be a pinprick on a map, most people didn't know that Hell even existed. Max Ridell wished he didn't.

He lay on his back in the middle of a dusty asphalt street, blood trickling from his nose. The hot July sun beat down, cooking the tar beneath him to blistering. To top it off, he thought one of his ribs was broken.

Groaning, he rolled over, spit dirt out of his mouth, and opened his eyes to see a pair of cowboy boots planted firmly apart an inch in front of him. Black, shiny—so shiny he could almost see his incipient black eye in them. His gaze crawled up long khaki-clad legs, past a decidedly female chest, to a woman's face.

Mirrored aviator sunglasses glinted in the bright sunlight. She stared down at him, her jaw moving in a slow, rhythmic motion, chewing what he hoped was gum. Her right hand rested on the butt of a businesslike .357 Magnum and a five-pointed star lay pinned to her khaki shirt above her left breast. A white felt cowboy hat sat on her head, covering short mahogany hair and shading much of her face, except for her wide, full mouth.

She opened that mouth and drawled, "You're under arrest."

Great. Busted by the Sheriff from Hell when he hadn't been half an hour in the armpit of the universe.

Max pulled himself painfully to his feet and stared at her, hands on his hips. She was tall for a woman, just a few inches shy of his own six feet one. "What the hell are you arresting *me* for? He started the fight." Max gestured toward the diner behind her. They both turned to see Max's attacker, Hugo the Hulk, rushing toward them, brandishing a vinyl café chair and cursing like a lunatic.

Damned if she didn't step back and give the sucker a clear shot at him. Max ducked the chair, kicked out and landed his foot dead-on in the guy's crotch. Even though Max wore running shoes rather than his customary boots, it should have leveled the guy. At least it made Hugo drop the chair. But judging by the hands getting acquainted with Max's neck, it hadn't fazed him much. None of the blows Max had landed earlier had bothered him.

Everything but the maniacal face with bulging eyes faded from Max's field of vision. The hands tightened. A roaring sounded in his ears as black dots danced before his eyes. His breath cut off.

Was the dumb broad just going to stand there and watch the turkey strangle him?

Dang, Grace O'Malley thought, frowning at the dust speckling her clean uniform. She ought to remember to stand farther back when folks went at it like that.

"I'll teach you to go after my woman, you sumbitch!" Jim Bob yelled.

That explained it, she mused. No telling if the dark-haired stranger had actually made a pass at Doreen, Jim Bob's girlfriend, but knowing Jim Bob's temper, all the other man would have had to do was speak to her and he'd be toast. Gracie watched with interest as the stranger's eyes glazed over and his face took on a blue tinge as Jim Bob squeezed tighter. Better do something or Jim Bob's latest victim would pass right out. She stepped to her patrol car a few paces away and reached inside for the fire extinguisher.

Since the stranger was getting the worst of it, she aimed the nozzle at Jim Bob's chest and let loose with a steady stream of CO_2. Satisfied, she watched the pair break apart. The stranger put his hand to his throat and sucked in air for all he was worth while Jim Bob stepped back, choking and coughing. As soon as Jim Bob got his breath back, he set up a storm of cussing. Gracie let him have it with the spray again until he shut up.

"Well, now," she said, waiting to see if she had their attention. They stared at her in silence, the stranger glaring at her while he wiped blood from his face and goop from his shirt. Even though she hadn't been aiming at him, he'd taken more than his share of foam. Tempted to laugh at the picture the two men presented, she figured she'd succeeded in snagging their notice.

"You're both under arrest. Disorderly conduct."

"What?" the masher shouted. "I didn't do anything except defend myself!"

At the same time Jim Bob yelled, "That prevert was hittin' on my woman!"

Motioning with the fire extinguisher hose, she paid them no mind. "Let's go," she said. They didn't look real cooperative, particularly Jim Bob, so she tucked the fire extinguisher under her arm and fondled the butt of her pistol before walking behind them and herding them toward the patrol car. "Spread 'em, fellas," she ordered as they reached the front quarter panel, "and keep your hands on the hood." Jim Bob, naturally, jerked around until she had to shove him up against the car. "Don't make me get ugly," she warned him as she patted him down.

"I don't have to make you get ugly, Sheriff," he said, turning his head to give her a nasty glare. "You already are ugly."

Gracie clenched her jaw so she wouldn't speak, not wanting him to know he'd touched a nerve. Ordinarily, she didn't let that kind of thing bother her, but something about the way Jim Bob always harped on her looks rankled. Besides, she might not be a raving beauty, but the face she saw in the mirror every morning wouldn't turn a person to stone, either. Shrugging off the insult, she pulled a set of handcuffs from her belt.

Jim Bob didn't tick her off major league until he spit at her. Lucky for him he missed. She slapped the cuffs on him and made sure she forgot to double lock them. The more he squirmed, and if she knew Jim Bob he'd fight every step of the way, the tighter the cuffs would get. He ought to know better by now than to rile her, but his middle name was Dumb. In the eighteen months she'd been sheriff of Bandido County, she'd run him in for everything from public intoxication, to petty theft, to domestic violence. Every time she hauled him in he gave her trouble, and every time, she turned it right back at him.

After shoving Jim Bob into the backseat, she turned her attention to the stranger. He was a big cuss, but he stood still and didn't hassle her, though she could tell he was spoiling to. With his jaw clenched tighter than an overwound watch spring, and that dark gleam in his pretty blue eyes, she'd have been scared witless had she been the type to frighten easy.

He was a stranger, though, so she took her time and was extra careful patting him down. You could never tell who was packing a weapon, and Gracie didn't intend to wind up dead due to carelessness.

Satisfied the newcomer was clean, she loaded him into the front seat and set off for the jail, a couple of miles away. Either the stranger was smarter than Jim Bob or he knew the process well enough to realize she could make him a whole lot more uncomfortable if she wanted. Could be he'd been arrested a time or two in the past.

Having heard it all before, Grace ignored the sewage spewing from Jim Bob's mouth and called the arrest in over the radio. Not only her tenure as sheriff, but six years as a city cop had guaranteed there wasn't much left that could shock her. After a while, though, she began to get irritated. The familiar throb of a headache pulled at her temples.

She hit the brakes hard. Jim Bob's head twanged against the cage separating the front seat from the back. "Darn," she drawled, glancing in the rearview mirror to see his eyes bugging out with fury. "Armadillo."

The man beside her bit off a curse but he didn't say anything else. Smart one, she thought again, feeling a little sorry for him. His head would've hit the dash, except his seat belt had jerked him back before that happened. It had tightened around him, of course, and she suspected he was pretty uncomfortable. She wished things were different, since she was nearly certain he hadn't started the fight, and besides, if anybody deserved to get punched, Jim Bob Mulligan did. But she couldn't prove her point to Bigmouth Mulligan without getting to the stranger as well.

Jim Bob kicked the back of her seat, causing a loose spring to poke her in the back. Hoping he'd quit when she didn't react, Gracie ignored him, but he kept on until the blasted coil dug into the small of her back and hurt like the dickens. Dadburnit! The kicking, along with his never ending garbage-mouth annoyed her to no end. She slammed on the brakes again.

"Dadgummit," she said cheerily, hearing Jim Bob's head rebound from the bars with a gratifying thud. "Another 'dillo. Mercy, that's two in one day."

"Do you have to do that?" the stranger snarled at her.

She shot him a sideways glance and bit the inside of her cheek to keep from smiling. With blood, dirt, and CO_2 dripping off him, he was a mess, but he was kind of cute all the same. With black hair and gorgeous blue eyes, she didn't doubt he'd clean up to be a nice-looking man. When he wasn't madder than a rained-on rooster, that is.

Wishing she hadn't quit smoking, she picked

up another piece of gum, unwrapped it, and popped it in her mouth. "Yep," she said.

They rode the entire way to jail with a brake check every minute or two. After the second one the stranger braced himself, but poor Jim Bob never did figure it out.

An hour later Gracie looked at the report she'd pulled up on Mr. Max Ridell, Jim Bob's sparring partner. No rap sheet. She was glad to know he hadn't been in trouble with the law, even if he did have a bad-boy look about him. Not even a traffic ticket, according to his driver's license record. Could be that bad-boy look had more to do with women than the law, she decided. When she had called Connie May Pritchett, the waitress at the diner and Gracie's best friend, to find out what had gone on from a bystander's viewpoint, Connie had told her he was a charmer.

Max Ridell had made a big mistake, trying to make time with Jim Bob's girl, but he wouldn't have known that. Lucky for him she hadn't put the two in the same cell or Jim Bob would've wiped the floor with him. He had the fact that he'd cooperated with her to thank for that.

Gracie decided it was time to talk to the man himself. Hopefully she'd be able to let him go, which would do two things. Tick Jim Bob off and save her from a lot of paperwork.

When she went to get him she found him pacing the concrete floor of his cell. She noticed he'd used the sink to clean up. The bruises, along with the swelled lip and Rudolph-red nose, highlighted those bad-boy looks, she thought, seeing his face clearly for the first time. Except he was no boy. He was definitely all man—every smooth muscled inch of him.

Whoa, Gracie, what's the matter with you? she asked herself. As a rule, she didn't drool over men. Never had before. She shook her head, taking a firm grip on her unruly thoughts.

"Come on, mister," she said as she unlocked the cell. "Let's see if we can figure out what to do with you." She led him to the gray metal booking desk, seating herself in the wooden rolling chair behind it.

"I can tell you that," he said, taking the other chair. "You can let me go. I keep telling you, I didn't start the fight."

She picked up a piece of spearmint gum and popped it into her mouth. Her jaw moved. The gum popped. "How about you tell me what happened," she said, leaning back in her chair and crossing her arms over her chest, getting comfortable.

He smiled—a roguish smile, full of promise— and Gracie knew that Connie had been right. A charmer, from the sky-blue of his eyes to the come-hither dimple in one bruised cheek.

"I must have interrupted a lover's quarrel," he said. "I asked one of the diner customers what was good to order. She made a couple of suggestions, and we hit it off. We started talking, just"—he spread his hands—"passing the time, you know?"

"Uh-huh."

"Her boyfriend," he continued, jerking a thumb at the drunk tank where Jim Bob resided, "didn't like it. Next thing I knew he was pounding my face in." He gingerly touched his finger to his swollen lip and frowned.

"Picking up strange women can be dangerous, all right," she said, as deadpan as she could get.

"I wasn't picking her up. All I did was talk to her."

He was trying to look innocent, but in Gracie's opinion he looked about as innocent as a dog on the dinner table. Right, she thought, a smile pulling at her mouth. "I know Doreen," she said, her eyes crinkling with her smile.

He grinned. "Okay, I'll admit, she's a looker."

"That's a fact." And boy howdy, could Doreen cause trouble when she wanted. Gracie's chair squeaked as she rocked forward to pick up a paper from the dented desktop. "I ran a check on you, Mr. Riii-dell," she said, drawing his last name out in her West Texas drawl. "No rap sheet."

"That's because I'm no criminal. I'm just a bystander who was attacked by a lunatic."

Since the word lunatic summed up Jim Bob to a tee, she let that pass. "Mind telling me what your business is in Hell?"

"I work for the Environmental Protection

Agency. I'm here to investigate the effects of the pollution from the *maquiladoras* on the Rio Grande and the land bordering the river."

She stared at him and blinked. "You're a biologist?" In her experience biologists were soft and stuffy, pale-faced bureaucrats. This man, with his tanned skin and hell-raiser looks, was no more her idea of an environmentalist than she was anyone's notion of a debutante.

"That's right." He shifted in the straight-backed chair and groaned. "I planned on contacting your office anyway to alert you to my presence and ask for your cooperation."

"Cooperation?" He'd need that all right. The ranchers around Hell didn't cotton to the EPA.

"Yes. I'm also investigating illegal dumping. If you know of any suspicious sites . . ." He let the sentence trail off and waited for her to speak.

"You want me to tell you if I know of anyone dumping illegally? Don't you think I'd have brought them in for questioning if I knew of anything like that going on?" Did he think she couldn't do her job?

He smiled at her again. He sure knew how to use that smile to his advantage. What would it be like if he smiled at her because he meant it and not because he wanted something?

"It's a big border," he said. "You can't be everywhere at once. Your office is small, isn't it?"

She took her time answering. "One deputy," she finally said, "and a few reserve officers.

They're there when we need them. A jailer and a dispatcher too. So tell me, Mr. Riii-dell, what exactly are you planning to do?"

"Call me Max." That lady-killer smile flashed again. "Take soil samples, water samples. Look around for anything suspicious."

"You plan on tromping around folks's ranch lands?" That ought to be something to watch.

"Yes. Is there a reason I shouldn't?"

She couldn't help grinning. "Not if you don't mind a seat full of buckshot."

"I've got every legal right to inspect these lands."

"Sounds like it," she agreed. An EPA agent. So he'd be sticking around awhile. The thought pleased her, though she couldn't have said why. She doubted she was Max Ridell's type.

The phone rang and she answered it. "O'Malley."

"Dogfight, Sheriff," a muffled voice said. "Out at the Washburn place."

"What?" Her grip tightened on the receiver. "Who's—?"

The line went dead. She barely stopped herself from slamming the phone down. Darn it! She'd warned those sons of guns that if she caught them fighting dogs again, she'd throw the whole library at them, but obviously her threats hadn't done anything to discourage them. Her stomach rolled when she thought about the animals. Gracie knew how vicious those fights could be.

"Sheriff? Are you all right?"

The deep male voice jerked her back to present business. Before she could leave she had to do something with Max Ridell. She didn't answer him, but rose and pulled a clear plastic bag out of the middle drawer of the desk and tossed his belongings down in front of him. "Check that it's all there and you're free to go."

"Thanks," he said, sifting through his things. He glanced up and smiled. "Looks like everything's here. But there's one problem, Sheriff. My truck's back at the diner. Is there a taxi service?"

The question made her forget about the dogfight long enough to laugh. "No taxis in Hell. Come on. I'll drop you by there on my way." She started for the door, expecting him to follow.

"Does this mean I can count on your help if I need it?"

She glanced back to see him slipping his wallet into the back pocket of his jeans, stretching the denim tight across his rear. She'd never really understood why Connie talked about men's rears being cute until that moment.

"Sheriff?"

She looked up at his face. The teasing glint in his eyes and the smile lifting one corner of his mouth indicated he'd noticed the direction of her gaze. Flushing, she glanced away, comforting herself with the certainty that she wasn't the first woman to look at him that way.

Belatedly remembering he'd asked for her help, she answered. "I imagine so."

"Thanks. I appreciate that."

A short while later she let him off at the diner, feeling vaguely regretful as she watched him walk away. She'd see him again, though, probably sooner than he expected. Knowing that the ranchers had as much use for the EPA as a cat does for a bath, she figured Max Ridell would be in hot water quicker than the flames of hell could scorch a tail feather.

TWO

"Atta girl, Izzy. You're just about well," Gracie said, giving the small black-and-white spaniel mix a last pat. "Tomorrow it's out with the troops."

Izzy thumped her tail and gazed at her with big brown soulful eyes. Gracie suspected that Izzy liked her position of honor, curled up as she was in a box in the kitchen, but the dog would adjust quickly enough to the rest of the animals.

Hearing a pounding at the back door followed by muffled cursing, she went to answer it. Connie May Pritchett blew in with a hug and a complaint.

"When are you going to train those damned rejects of yours, Gracie?" she asked. "Look at my skirt!" She swept a hand over the garment, long red nails gleaming. "It's ruined!"

"Be reasonable, Connie." She glanced down at her own jeans and faded blue T-shirt. "You know better than to wear anything nice out here. Besides, it'll wash." Except if Connie shrank that flimsy thing she called a skirt any more, Gracie would have to arrest her for indecent exposure. But there was no changing Connie, so Gracie didn't try.

Making herself at home with the ease of someone who'd been to grade school with her, Connie headed straight for the refrigerator. "So tell me about yesterday," she said, pulling out a pitcher of tea and pouring a couple of glasses. "Why in the world did you arrest both of them? I told you Jim Bob started it."

"Didn't have a choice. Couldn't bring Jim Bob in without bringing the other one too." Gracie picked up her tea and added, "I'm surprised you weren't over here last night wanting to know everything I could tell you." Not to mention everything she couldn't tell her. Connie was a gossip with a capital *G*, though she never meant any harm.

"I had plans," Connie said.

"With Reese?" Gracie asked, referring to her friend's fiancé. "I thought the Chapmans were busy with those new cattle?"

Connie flung up a hand. "Don't talk about cattle. I'm so sick of hearing about that damned ranch, I don't know what to do. I want to know about this man. Heard him telling Doreen his name was Max and he was going to be in town awhile."

Dodged that question, Grace thought. She

suspected things weren't going well for Connie and Reese, but her friend would talk to her when she was ready and not before. "Looks that way. Max Ridell," she said. "He's a biologist with the EPA."

"A *biologist*?" Connie stared at her. "Didn't look like a biologist to me. More like— hmm . . ." She tapped a finger on her temple, narrowing her eyes. "I'll have to think about that. He's no cowboy, that's for sure. Looks like he could be a lot of fun, if you know what I mean." She raised her eyebrows and wiggled them suggestively.

Gracie had an idea, though not from personal experience. She suspected her friend was right about Max Ridell being fun, but Connie was wrong about him not being a cowboy. A slow smile spread over her face. He'd look right at home in boots and a Stetson. "Prettiest blue eyes I ever saw," she said, thinking aloud. Not to mention that come-and-get-me smile of his. He'd been nice, too, which had surprised her considering she'd just thrown him in jail. Most people reacted like Jim Bob and cussed her out. She appreciated a man who could hold his temper.

"Gracie! I've never heard you talk about a man's eyes before."

Startled out of her reverie, she glanced at her friend. "Sure I have." She frowned, then took a sip of tea.

"Not with that goofy smile on your face."

"It wasn't a goofy smile." Okay, so maybe it was, she admitted silently. "For Pete's sake, Connie, I'm not blind. He's a good-looking guy. So what?"

Connie cocked her head and studied Gracie, her expression giving her the look of an eager robin waiting for a worm. Her teased red hair only strengthened the impression.

"Are you interested in this man?"

Was she? "Maybe," Gracie said. "Not that it matters. Look who he was trying to pick up."

"Oh, Doreen." Connie dismissed the prettiest woman in town with a sniff and a wave of her hand. "If you ask me, she was a sight more taken with him than he was with her. Don't talk that way, Gracie. You're too hard on yourself."

"Nope." Gracie shook her head and rose. "I'm a realist. And this realist needs to feed the mob. Come talk to me while I do."

Connie followed her out the door, scolding all the way to the barn. The pack's enthusiasm made for slow going. Between swatting at noses and dodging smelly obstacles, Connie managed to fit in a week's worth of nagging about Gracie's low opinion of herself, finishing up with, "If you'd give a man half a chance instead of automatically assuming he couldn't possibly want—"

"Con," Gracie interrupted, "we've been through this before. Men—most men, anyway—don't see a woman when they look at me. They see the sheriff, or a friend, or even an enemy, but they don't see a woman."

It didn't particularly bother her, because to tell the truth, she hadn't yet met a man she thought would be worth the trouble that was sure to follow falling in love, judging from most of her friends' love lives. Still, her own parents had had a good marriage, and something about Max Ridell made her question that belief. It wasn't just his looks, though he was cute enough. And it wasn't the fact that he'd been decent to her when she'd arrested him, though that had helped. Maybe—

"Only the fools around here can't see you as a woman," Connie said, intruding on her thoughts again. "They've known you forever and still don't have a clue about the real you. Stop that, Caesar!" She broke off to shove at the Great Dane poking his nose up under her skirt.

Gracie bit her lip to keep from laughing. "Sorry, Con. But he always has liked you. See, he's trying to apologize."

"He's sorry, all right," Connie said, glaring at him.

In an effort to look properly penitent, the big dog had rolled over on his back and was waving his paws in apology. "It's rude to go about sticking your nose in people's—Oh, never mind. I'm talking about men, not one-eyed Goliaths."

When Connie launched into a lecture there was no stopping her, Gracie thought, and resigned herself to hearing it.

"I'll tell you what it is about men," Connie went on. "You have to beat them over the head with a stick to get their attention. Why don't you ever dress like a girl? You'd be surprised at what a short skirt can accomplish." She wiggled her hips for emphasis.

Gracie snorted. "I'd look pretty silly feeding these guys in heels and a skirt. Besides, I'd be six feet tall if I wore heels." Hauling out a fifty-pound sack of dog food, she pulled the seal-string and poured the contents into a large trash can. Then she grabbed a scoop and started dumping the kernels into smaller pans. Her troops went through dog food like Sherman had gone through Georgia, but with twelve, no make that thirteen—she'd forgotten about the newest addition—dogs, it took a lot to feed them.

"Some men like tall women," Connie argued. "Besides, that's just an excuse and you know it. Your boots make you taller, and you wear them all the time. Why do you waste yourself out here on all these"—she gestured at the adoring mob of furry bodies, slopping doggie breath and dog hair everywhere—"rejects? You have so much to give—"

"Why don't you feed the cats instead of nagging me to death?" Grace asked, finally getting irritated.

Grabbing the sack of kitty feed, Connie did as she was told. But she kept on yakking, which didn't surprise Gracie. Sometimes she wondered if Connie had nagged her first husband into a divorce, but she squelched the thought because she loved her friend, even with her faults.

"What about Bill?" Connie asked. "Wasn't that his name? You know, the cop you dated for a while when you were in El Paso. He thought of you as a woman, didn't he?"

It took her a minute to remember who Connie was talking about. "Oh, him. Yeah, I guess he did." Her eyes crinkled as she thought about it. "He was a nice guy, but I don't think he was any more fired up about me than I was about him."

And that was the problem, she mused. She'd dated a few men, mostly other cops, between leaving home and returning, but the relationships had all been more lukewarm than fiery. She had never wanted to go to bed with a man simply because neither of them had anything better to do. It seemed to her that making love ought to be more . . . well, more important than that. When the men found out she wasn't interested in sleeping with them, they hightailed it out of her life faster than a prairie fire with a tailwind.

"So everybody runs across a few duds now and then," Connie said. "Try for once, instead of giving up before you even get started. Do something about this new fellow. He's going to need all the friends he can get, once everyone finds out what he's doing here."

That was true, Gracie acknowledged. The ranchers thought that environmentalists made for good buzzard bait and not much else. Funny, Max Ridell didn't strike her as a typical EPA agent. She couldn't put her finger on why, though. But as for Connie's great idea of her trying to get his notice—nah, it wouldn't work. He'd been nice to her because he wanted out of jail and he wasn't dumb. Still, being the object of Max Ridell's undivided attention was a tempting thought.

An hour later, Connie left, claiming to have a date with Reese. That must have been a lie, though. Half an hour after that Grace got a call from Reese, and it was plain from his conversation that Connie wasn't with him. He was calling about a trespasser on the ranch, and to tell her his father had taken off after the man with his gun.

Poor Max, Gracie thought, grinning as she strapped on her belt. Since the Chapmans' land bordered the river, she'd bet the ranch he was the trespasser. He hadn't gotten a very warm welcome in Hell.

Ass-deep in the Rio Grande, Max cursed the day he'd agreed to take this assignment. The old man stood six feet away from him on the bank of the river, the business end of a shotgun pointed at Max's chest. If he moved the rancher would plug him as full of holes as a sieve.

One more time, he tried to reason with him. "Mr. Chapman, all I want to do is take a few soil samples." And look around for halfway stations

Ye Olde English Christmas Madrigal Feaste

December 7, 1996
6:30 PM
(seating begins at 6:00 PM)

Endwell United Methodist Church
3301 Watson Blvd.
Endwell, NY 13760

$ 17.50

9A

PRINCESS

ANDREA HOWARD

while he was at it, but the old geezer didn't need to know that.

"You got no business nosing around on my property. I don't give a rat's be-damned what you want."

So much for his legal right to be there. The wiry old goat looked like the type to shoot first and ask questions later. It irked Max to think that he was in exactly the position Sheriff Grace O'Malley had predicted, with that surprisingly lush mouth of hers curving upward as she spoke. "A seat full of buckshot" looked like the *best* he could hope for at this point. She'd be rolling on the ground laughing if she could see him now.

Speak of the devil, he thought as movement beyond the old man caught his eye. Or in this case, the Sheriff from Hell. Wasn't that her patrol car topping the rise? He squinted into the gathering twilight as the white, boxy-shaped vehicle drew closer, throwing up a cloud of dust on the sorry excuse for a road that bordered the rancher's field.

Chapman turned around to look behind him. "Ha! Now we'll see. Here comes the sheriff. Gracie'll arrest your tail right quick."

Just dandy, Max thought. Bad enough to be on the receiving end of a shotgun, but why did Grace O'Malley have to show up? He doubted she'd arrest him, but this was the second time she'd caught him looking like an incompetent fool and he didn't much care for the experience.

The patrol car ground to a halt. She got out, glanced at Max, then ambled over toward Chapman. Though slow, her stride was sure and confident. Competent, he thought, watching her. Instead of a uniform, she wore jeans. But even without the gun belt and cowboy hat she'd have looked like a sheriff. A take-charge kind of woman. She'd handled Jim Bob, she'd handled him, and he didn't doubt she'd handle Chapman as well. But how?

Reaching the rancher, she tipped her hat and said, her voice a sociable drawl, "Evenin', Mr. Chapman. Reese tells me you're having a little problem here."

"Not a problem. I fixed it for the most part, and I'm waiting for him to leave." Chapman lowered the gun long enough to add, "How about you arrest him and save me some buckshot?"

"Well now, it might not be that simple."

Thank God for sensible women, Max thought. His best course, he decided, would be to keep his mouth shut and let her handle the matter, though it went against the grain to do so. Fisting his hands beneath the water's surface, he waited.

"My land, my gun," Chapman said, "He ain't welcome. Sounds simple to me. Arrest the bugger."

"Did he tell you what he wanted?"

"Said he was a damned biologist with the damned EPA." With his free hand, Chapman hitched up his overalls. "I didn't need to hear more." Raising his gun again, he aimed it at Max.

"Well now." She took off her hat, ran a hand through her short dark hair, replaced the hat. "I'm afraid that isn't all there is to it. You can't stop the EPA from being on your land."

"Wanna bet? My shotgun says different."

She ignored the threat and continued as if he hadn't spoken. "My dispatcher put in a whistle to the EPA. She's supposed to call and tell me if he checks out. If he does, and I expect he will, you've got to let him do his job, Mr. Chapman."

"What if I don't?" The old man thrust out his whiskered chin belligerently. The gun didn't waver from its position.

Max took comfort from the fact that the gathering darkness made it unlikely Chapman could see well enough to hit him.

The sheriff shook her head regretfully. "Then I'm sorry as can be, but I'll have to take you in."

He'd been glaring fixedly at Max, but at that comment he jerked his head around to stare at her. "Grace O'Malley, I can't believe you're talking to me like this. You've known me all your life. What's got into you? Your daddy would never have acted this way."

"You're wrong, Mr. Chapman." Her voice changed, hardened. "My father would've run you in because he did his job. And that's what I'll do if I have to."

She planted her feet apart in a now-familiar

stance. Not threatening, but determined. It made those long legs of hers look even longer—and definitely female, definitely enticing.

"Knew no good would come of electing a female sheriff," Chapman muttered, but he lowered his gun. "Might just rethink my vote come next election."

"Your privilege," she said. Then she spoke to Max. Aside from the brief glance when she'd arrived, it was the first good look she'd taken at him.

He could still see well enough to note the smile tugging at her mouth, and it fanned the embers of his already strained temper.

"You can come on out now, Mr. Riii-dell. We'll just wait until I get the nod on your credentials."

Gritting his teeth so he wouldn't tell her to stuff it, Max climbed out and started for his truck. Full of sludge and water, his shoes squished unpleasantly as he walked. His jeans clung to his legs, wet, clammy, and feeling like they'd been dipped in lead. Probably had. God only knew what was in that water.

"Where are you going, Mr. Ridell?" she called after him.

Chapman, his voice rising, said, "See? He's gettin' away! Arrest the bugger, I say! Shoot him!"

Max turned and glared at her. "I've got papers in my truck to prove my business here. Besides, I told you yesterday what I was here for."

"Yep." She nodded agreeably. "But I've got to

have confirmation. Not that I don't believe you," she added. "Something like that's pretty simple to check."

Hanging on to his temper by the tips of his fingers, Max stalked to the truck, jerked open the door, and popped open the glove compartment.

"Got a permit for that gun?" her voice asked near his shoulder.

He turned around to find her right behind him. He'd had no idea she could move that quickly or silently. She wrinkled her nose and stepped back a pace, not that he blamed her. Stinkweed smelled better than he did right then. He didn't want to think about the toxins that might have entered his system. "Here are my credentials," he said, handing them to her and silently thanking his boss for insisting he have the real things. "And here's the permit for the gun."

It wasn't quite dark, but she pulled out her flashlight and shined it on the papers, taking her sweet time perusing them. Max bit his tongue, ground his teeth, and waited.

"Everything looks in order," she finally said, and turned to the rancher. "Mr. Chapman, looks like you're out of luck. I couldn't find anything wrong with his credentials."

"What? You mean I've got to let the dirty bastard nose around on my property?" he demanded incredulously. "Never heard of such a thing."

" 'Fraid so," she said, warm understanding in her voice. "But I'm sure Mr. Ridell would be willing to come back tomorrow." She looked at him and raised an eyebrow in silent question.

Max ground his teeth again and counted to ten. That didn't accomplish anything, so he counted to fifty. Losing his temper wouldn't help—the sheriff was his only ally. Besides, she hadn't sent him into the water. She might have predicted it, but she hadn't actually done it. Still, he didn't like being rescued by a woman, sheriff or not. Call him macho, but it galled the hell out of him. Twice, she'd come to his rescue. Twice he'd looked like a fool.

"Perfectly willing," he gritted out.

Chapman stomped off, shotgun over his shoulder, muttering darkly as he went.

The sheriff contemplated Max, her mouth curving upward, her gaze taking in every miserable detail of his appearance. Her big brown eyes danced with enjoyment, yanking his chain still further.

"Glad you find this so amusing, Sheriff."

"From my viewpoint it is pretty funny. And you do smell kinda like a polecat-sprayed dog. Hope it fades faster than skunk smell does."

He unclenched his jaw to speak. "It might, assuming I could shower."

"Why can't you shower?"

"Because nothing in this godforsaken part of the state works right. The water's off at the motel. God knows when they'll get it fixed. The owner said the well pump went out, and they didn't appear to be in any hurry to fix it."

She nodded understandingly. "That would be because the pump repairman is hard to get ahold of. It's a shame for you, though."

He glared at her, not believing her sympathetic tone for a moment. "Yeah, isn't it? I'm sure it's breaking your heart."

She stared at him, not saying anything. After a long pause, she spoke. "You can clean up at my house. Hell hasn't been too hospitable to you, has it?"

Max laughed, surprised at the offer. "Thanks. No, hospitable isn't the word I'd use."

"Jim Bob was partly your fault, you know. If you hadn't been trying to make time with his girl—"

He interrupted her. "All I did was talk to the woman."

"So you said." Her eyes glimmered with amusement before sobering. "But as for this other, the ranchers have good reason to dislike the EPA. No, better make that hate their guts."

"Why's that?"

She frowned, puzzled. "The bug thing, remember? You folks durn near bankrupted three fourths of the families around here with that foolishness. As if things hadn't been bad enough before that with the price of cattle dropping to rock bottom."

Bug thing? Bankruptcy? What the hell was she

talking about? Clearly something he was supposed
to know. "I'm here on a different matter. I don't
plan to bankrupt anyone. I just want to do my
job." And get the hell out of Hell.

"That's what the other fellows said. And look
what happened."

Research, you idiot, Max told himself. He'd
better call the captain—or the EPA—that night
and find out what the "bug thing" was. "You obviously agree with them."

She rolled her shoulder. "People and their
livelihoods are more important than bugs, in my
book. But try telling that to the EPA."

Turning her back on him, she started walking
toward her car. Still ticked off, he watched her go.
He had to admit he liked the way she moved.
He'd never seen anything quite like that walk of
hers. Slow and almost . . . sultry, he decided,
though he hadn't thought her a sultry kind of
woman.

"You can follow me in your truck," she said
over her shoulder.

Thank God something had finally gone right.
Her hospitality made it easier on him than he'd
expected. Of course, that was because she thought
he was an EPA agent. He slammed the truck door,
wondering what Sheriff O'Malley would do if she
found out he was a Texas Ranger—and that she
was under investigation.

THREE

Gracie stood under her porch light, watching Max Ridell walk toward her. Even with half a dozen animals getting in his way, he had a long-legged cowboy kind of stride she'd wager earned him a second glance or two. The dogs leaped about, barking their joy, except Caesar and Red, who'd rolled onto their backs with their legs in the air, like they always did when anyone new came around. The cats wove around her legs, meowing. She wondered what he'd make of her menagerie.

"Oh, you big baby," she said to Caesar, one of the presumed dead. "This is Max. He won't hurt you." Glancing at Max, she half-smiled. "I didn't think you'd mind. Just tell them to sit. Mostly they listen."

Max patted Boo, a three-legged black-and-tan hound dog, and grinned. "They couldn't make these clothes smell any worse."

Caesar, apparently deciding the newcomer was no threat, waltzed over, reared up, and planted his huge paws on the visitor's chest.

"Sit," Max told him.

The big dummy barked and licked his cheek. "Caesar, get down," Gracie said, struggling with laughter again. "Sorry. He's one who mostly doesn't."

Max laughed, firmly yet gently pushing the dog away to follow her inside. "So what's this? A home for wayward dogs?"

"Folks around here call them Gracie's rejects." Glancing at Izzy, she remembered how pitiful the spaniel had been when she first came compared to how good she looked now. "To me they're just animals who need love and attention."

She turned away, saying, "I'll show you the bathroom. If you want to give me those clothes, I'll wash them. My father's clothes might fit you."

"Thanks. Are you sure he won't mind?"

"Don't see why. He passed away a couple of years ago. Might as well put them to good use."

"I really appreciate this."

She nodded. "Go on and get out of those clothes and I'll start them washing."

He shut the bathroom door. As she waited, she heard him swearing under his breath. Wet jeans were the dickens to get out of, she thought, and grinned.

A minute or so later the door opened, his arm extended, and he dropped the filthy mess into her hands. "Watch out something doesn't jump out and bite you. Not that I expect there was anything alive in that water."

She laughed and left to start the load.

Glad she'd never brought herself to get rid of all her father's clothes, Gracie rummaged in the back closet. She held up a pair of jeans and tried to decide if they'd fit Max. It was her daddy's jeans or hers, and she knew for a fact hers wouldn't work. The shirts, though, would never do. Her father had been thinner toward the end, not nearly as big as Max. Maybe she had something in her closet.

Finally she discovered a white cotton T-shirt she wore as a nightshirt that she thought might fit him. The idea of Max Ridell wearing one of her nightshirts seemed awfully . . . intimate. As if using her shower wasn't? At the thought of him in the shower, she blushed. Gracie, my girl, get ahold of yourself, she scolded silently.

She paused outside the bathroom door and heard no water running. "Max?" she called, and knocked. "Here are those clothes. I'll just leave—"

The door swung open, and her words died in her throat. Steam rising about him, he stood there wearing nothing but a white towel wrapped around his lean waist. Over six feet of bare-chested, clean-smelling, tanned, healthy male, not half a foot away from her.

With her gaze riveted to his smooth, muscled

chest, he flat took her breath away. Lord help her, she felt as dizzy as if she'd just ridden the tilt-a-whirl at the fairgrounds. She'd seen men's bare chests before, hadn't she? But they hadn't looked like this man's. No chest she'd ever seen had looked like Max Ridell's. So broad . . . so masculine . . . so downright beautiful . . .

"Sheriff?"

Her gaze lifted to his face. A face still bruised, but not nearly as red and swollen as it had been at the jail, it fairly shouted, "Watch out for this one!" She swallowed hard and blinked. "G-Gracie," she stuttered. "Call me Gracie."

Realizing she still held the clothes, she thrust them toward him. "Here. They might not fit," she said, glancing at his chest again and doing her best not to look any farther down for fear she'd faint. Hastily, she dragged her gaze back up to his face.

His mouth curved upward as he reached to take her father's jeans and her own nightshirt from her. Their hands brushed. Her skin tingled, her stomach flip-flopped. The scent of soap, and of him, taunted her senses. Caught, she stared into those wickedly smiling blue eyes and wondered what it would be like to lay her palm against the warm, golden skin of his chest.

"Thank you. Gracie," he said, his deep voice laced with amusement.

She fled to the kitchen.

Safely away from him, her brain began to

function again. What was wrong with her? He's just a man, Gracie, she told herself. Nothing to get exercised about.

She added a little salt to the vegetable beef soup she was making. Soup, she thought, disgusted. Why couldn't she have decided to cook something more . . . exciting? And what if she had? It would take more than good cooking to interest a man like him.

What had he thought of her, staring at him as she had? From the gleam in those gorgeous eyes, she bet he'd known exactly what she'd been thinking.

Cut it out, Gracie, she told herself. *You no more fit with him than tofu would at a cattleman's ball.*

By the time he came in a few minutes later, she'd lectured herself enough so she thought she could handle him—and herself. Besides, he'd be wearing clothes now.

"I don't suppose you'll take further pity on me and feed me, will you?" he said.

Bowl of soup in hand, she turned around—and darn near dropped the soup. Her shirt fit him decently enough. A little snug, but that only played up the muscles of his chest and arms, as if she needed help noticing. But the jeans—Lordy Pete, even Connie didn't wear her jeans that tight. Struck dumb, Gracie hastily set the bowl on the table and pointed at a chair.

He grinned and took a seat. "Considering the fit of these jeans, I probably shouldn't, but that soup smells too good to resist. Guess I'll just have to live dangerously."

She gave a strangled groan and turned back to the stove, blindly filling another soup bowl. *He* was living dangerously? What about her? Fantasies about herself and a man like him would lead nowhere, she was sure of that. But that didn't stop her from having them.

Max left the sheriff's house well satisfied with the evening. Though he hadn't learned much he didn't already know, he had established a friendly relationship with Gracie. And unless he'd forgotten how to read a woman, she wouldn't mind getting on even friendlier terms. If her office, and therefore the sheriff herself, hadn't been under investigation for running a smuggling ring, he'd have been tempted to do something about that spark of longing he'd seen in her eyes.

No law against thinking about it, though. At first glance he'd have described Gracie as plain, but it hadn't taken him long to change that opinion. One look at her smiling, her big brown eyes sparkling with amusement, had wiped all thoughts of plain out of his head. She wasn't beautiful, but she had something more unusual, more intriguing. Character—that she had in spades.

Max's tastes didn't normally run to character in a woman. No, his usual style, at least since his wife's death, ran more to beauty than brains and not too many morals to quibble about. None of that seemed to describe Grace O'Malley. Besides, it didn't matter a damn how much she intrigued him. He wasn't there to sleep with her, he was there to investigate her. The sooner he remembered that, the better for both of them.

Someone in this godforsaken place was part of that ring, he'd bet his badge on it. But Grace O'Malley—a smuggler of illegal aliens? She didn't seem the type to bring human beings across the border packed seventeen to a Porta Potti. It might be as simple as looking the other way while someone else did the actual work, though. But even that didn't seem in line with what he'd learned about Gracie so far.

The next day Max hit the diner at lunchtime, figuring if Hell was like most small towns, the diner would be a hub of activity.

Some hub, he thought, looking around from his seat at the dingy white counter. Not much of a crowd that day. The chatty redheaded waitress he'd met his first day was spending most of her time flirting with the brawny deputy instead of refilling the coffee cups of the few other diners.

Deputy Leroy Dunn. His other prime suspect. The burly, dark-haired deputy seemed typical of a number of small town law enforcement officials that he had met. A little full of himself, Max thought, overhearing snatches of conversation between Dunn and the redhead. That didn't make Dunn guilty of anything but conceit, though. Too bad. If it had to be Gracie or the deputy, he'd much rather it was Dunn.

Deciding he might as well attempt the Chapmans' ranch again, Max signaled for his check.

Connie, the waitress, slapped it down with a cheery, "There you go, sugar," and waited for him to pay.

Max reached for his wallet and came up empty. Frowning, he checked his other pocket. Nothing. He'd had it at Gracie's the night before, he knew. Instead of dirtying up his freshly washed and dried jeans, he'd carried the wallet to the truck in his hand. Had he left it in his motel room? No, he distinctly remembered putting it in his right hip pocket that morning because he'd had to reload it after washing it off and spreading everything out to dry the previous night.

"Something wrong?" the waitress asked, her head tilted inquisitively.

"Uh, I can't seem to find my wallet."

She raised one slim eyebrow significantly and waited.

Max felt his face flush. Damn, what was it about this town that jinxed him? "I know what it looks like, but I swear I had it in my pocket this morning. If you'll let me run over to the motel, I'll get—"

"This tree hugger trying to stiff you, Connie?"

The question came from the deputy sheriff,

hitching his pants up and puffing out his chest in an official manner.

For a moment, Connie seemed uncertain, but apparently decided in Max's favor. "He's just lost his wallet."

"Girl, you are so naive." To Max he said, "Pay up, bug lover, or your ass is goin' to jail."

"No need for that, Leroy. He said he'd get the money. It's only a four-dollar check, anyway."

"Still against the law."

"If the waitress doesn't have a problem with it—" Max began.

"The waitress ain't the owner," Deputy Dunn interrupted.

"So ask the owner," Max said. "For God's sake, we're not talking about armed robbery. It's a four-dollar check."

"Owner's gone fishin'," Dunn said, smiling. "Ain't that just the luck. Are you resisting arrest, boy?"

Wouldn't he just love that? Max thought. Obviously the turkey was spoiling for a fight—to impress the redhead with his law-enforcing prowess, no doubt. Max counted silently, reminding himself he'd solve nothing by antagonizing the deputy. God, this job was hard on his temper. When he thought he had it under control he spoke. "Don't you have to arrest me before I can resist? I wasn't aware I'd been arrested."

"We'll settle that right quick, then. You're under arrest for theft, bug lover."

Fifteen minutes later, the cell door clanged shut behind Max with a disturbing familiarity. For the second time in three days, he'd landed in the holding cell of Bandido County jail on a damned misdemeanor charge. He sat on the cold, unforgiving stone bench lining one wall and considered his surroundings. Luxurious they weren't. A stainless steel commode and sink were the only other fixtures in the cell. Max prepared himself for a long, boring wait.

He'd been there about half an hour when Grace O'Malley walked in. She stopped at the door to the holding tank. "Can't you stay out of jail?"

He grinned, oddly cheered to see her. "Apparently not."

"Did you try to stiff the diner?"

He rose and walked to the door. "No, I lost my wallet."

"Then why did—oh, never mind. Leroy must've gotten a bug up his nose for some reason."

Hands on the bars, he nodded. "I think he wanted to impress the redhead. I made an easy target."

She stared at him for a moment, then smiled. Damn, she had a cute smile. He liked it—more than he should.

"I wouldn't call you an easy target," she said. "But . . . impress the redhead? You mean the waitress? Connie?"

"That's what it looked like to me."

She shook her head, looking puzzled before she shrugged it off. "You sure have a way with attracting trouble. C'mon." She opened the cell door and led him past the booking desk where the jailer dozed, into another room. Her office, he assumed as he took the wooden straight-backed chair she waved at. "Leroy," she called from the doorway. "Could you come in here please?"

Deputy Dunn didn't look too happy to see either of them when he walked in.

"Sheriff, what are you doing here? Why did you get this tree hugger out of the holding cell?"

Gracie rested a hip on the desk, crossed her arms over her chest, and looked her deputy up and down. "Connie called me. Leroy, you've just got to take time to think things through. Why did you arrest him"—she nodded her head toward Max—"when Connie said it wasn't a problem?"

"He broke the law," the deputy insisted. "I had a right."

"I lost my wallet," Max said. "Last I heard that wasn't a crime. Not my crime, anyway."

"You got no call to interfere here, Sheriff," Dunn said, ignoring Max after flashing him a brief look of loathing.

Gracie shook her head. "I'd just as soon I didn't have to interfere, but I can't have you throwing folks in jail for no good reason. Didn't you notice Maude was there?"

Maude? Max wondered. What the hell was she

talking about? Judging by the flush in the deputy's cheeks, the question meant something to him, though.

"No. Just because—"

Gracie reached in her back pocket, pulled out something that looked a whole lot like Max's wallet, and tossed it onto the desk beside her. "We've talked about this before. Always check Maude first. I stopped by the diner before I came here. Maude was still there."

Dunn stared at the wallet, his face growing redder as the silence lengthened.

"Excuse me," Max said, "but who the hell is Maude and what does she have to do with anything?"

"Maude Abbott is the postmistress," Gracie told him. "And—well, it's like this. Maude's got a little problem borrowing things that don't belong to her."

Max stared at her blankly. "Borrowing?" he repeated.

A ghost of a smile on her mouth, Gracie added, "But she always gives them back. All you have to do is ask."

"Let me get this straight. The postmistress is a kleptomaniac?"

Her lips twitched. "Yep. That's what they call it."

"And she liberated my wallet from my hip pocket while I ate lunch?"

Gracie nodded ruefully. " 'Fraid so. Everybody around here knows if they miss something, just ask Maude." She shot Dunn an admonishing glance. "Except Leroy must have forgotten this time."

Of course, Max thought. Hell would have a kleptomaniac postmistress. Perfectly reasonable.

"You can press charges if you want," Gracie said, "but remember, you did get your wallet back."

"Thanks to you. And no thanks to Deputy Dog there. He wanted to lynch me over a four-dollar check."

Gracie bit her lip, trying not to laugh, Max suspected. "Leroy, I think we owe Mr. Ridell here an apology."

She'd included herself in that, but Dunn was bound to be furious with her, Max thought. Still, she was his boss and hadn't left him a choice that Max could see. Sheriff O'Malley was surprisingly smooth.

"Sorry for the misunderstanding," Dunn mumbled, catching Max's eye with a baleful glare.

One new enemy, Max thought. "Not a problem," he said. "And I won't press charges."

"Thank you."

Gracie's voice was soft and appreciative. And husky. With very little effort it brought to mind hot summer nights, tangled sheets, sweaty bodies. Max stared at her, caught in her gentle gaze.

"I'm going out on patrol," Dunn said, his harsh voice breaking the spell.

"Sure thing, Leroy." Gracie watched him go, then turned back to Max. "Boy howdy, he was as mad as a fox in an empty henhouse. If he'd just think for once before he hauled off and—"

The phone jangled, and she stretched across the desk to get it. Her position brought several inappropriate ideas to Max's mind. What was it about this woman?

"O'Malley." Frowning, she said, "All right, I'll send Dunn out there."

"Can you wait a minute before you go?" she asked Max as she cradled the receiver. "I've got to go talk to the dispatcher but it won't take long."

"Sure. No hurry." About time he had some luck, he thought, glad of the opportunity to do a little snooping. No chance for a serious search, since he damn sure didn't want to get caught with his hands in her drawers. A glance at the calendar on her desk granted him a few names, times, and meeting places. Also written under that day's date was the word "worms."

Worms?

"Thanks for waiting," Gracie said as she came back in. "I appreciate your not pressing charges against Maude. I'd hate like the dickens to bring her in. Probably give her a heart attack."

"Just point her out to me so I'll know to keep my distance."

"Deal," she said, offering him a generous smile.

When she smiled and her eyes sparkled like

they were doing now, he forgot that he preferred beautiful, brainless women. Not in any hurry to leave her, he cast around for a way to prolong the contact—for the investigation's sake, of course. "What's there to do around here after dark?"

"There's a movie theater about thirty miles away. Bingo every Thursday at the school cafeteria. And there's a pool hall down on Main Street. Only place around you can get a beer."

And it ought to be a good place to get information. "A cold one sounds good to me. How about a game of pool tonight? I'll spring for the beer too."

"You want—you're asking me—" Breaking off, she stared at him. She looked stunned.

"Hey, I'm not out of line, am I? Stepping on some guy's toes?" His preliminary investigation of her hadn't turned up any husband, but that didn't mean she wasn't seeing someone. Given her reaction, he figured he'd better ask.

"Out of line?" She blinked, and an odd look crossed her face. "Uh, no."

Something told him Gracie didn't date much. "So, how about it? Are you busy tonight?"

Laughter wiped the dazed look from her eyes. "I was planning on worming the dogs, but I do believe I'd rather shoot pool."

Worms. He should've figured that after seeing that Noah's Ark of hers. "Okay, I'll pick you up at seven-thirty. Unless Chapman shoots me when I go back this afternoon."

She smiled. "That'd put a damper on the evening, now wouldn't it? Don't worry. Mr. Chapman blusters a lot, but he won't really shoot you."

"Good thing one of us is sure of that," Max said, and walked out.

FOUR

Max spent three hours that afternoon tromping around the Chapmans' land without finding much. There were some obvious signs of people crossing the river, but he didn't doubt every ranch along the water had signs of that. He didn't find a hint of halfway stations where the coyotes, the men who brought the aliens across the border, could stash their human cargo before they were transported farther inland. Still, it was too early to get discouraged. He hadn't by any means covered the entire border or even the portion that adjoined the Chapmans' land.

Although the Chapmans weren't the only people with land along the river, Max couldn't muster a lot of enthusiasm for checking the other ranches in the area. Considering Gracie's comments and his own subsequent call to the EPA about "the bug thing," he figured that the majority of the ranchers in Bandido County would be just as welcoming as old man Chapman had been. As Gracie had told him, the EPA's attempt a few years earlier to protect an endangered species of beetle had nearly bankrupted the entire county. At the rate he was gaining information, he ought to be in Hell forever.

By 7:30 that evening, having gotten a message that Gracie would meet him, Max sat at the bar in Burt's pool hall nursing a cold draft beer and waiting for her to show up. It was early yet for the bar crowd, and the clientele consisted of some old geezers playing dominoes.

Max considered again that he and his captain might have picked the wrong cover for his investigation. Sure, the EPA had jurisdiction and a legal right to go on any land they pleased, but what difference did that make when the ranchers all wanted to shoot him on sight? He needed to be able to talk to them, he needed an in with the community. It looked to him like getting to know Grace O'Malley was the perfect solution to his problem. And he had to admit, the idea of knowing Gracie better was no hardship.

Caught up in his musings, he didn't realize Gracie had arrived until he heard her name called out.

"Hey, Gracie, how's it goin'?" Burt, owner and bartender, picked up a glass and filled it with a pale yellow liquid.

"Can't complain, Burt," she said, her gaze

skimming the place until she caught sight of Max. A slow grin spread over her face. Obviously one of the regulars, she accepted the glass Burt handed her without even glancing at it.

The fact that she was glad to see him shouldn't have mattered to Max, but he found that he liked it. Appreciatively, he watched her walk toward him with that measured stride of hers. She wore black jeans, boots, and a button-down green satin shirt that made her look like a cowgirl. Which, he supposed, she was. The clothes suited her, the color of the blouse bringing out the warm mahogany shades of her hair and the fair cast of her skin, and the jeans making her look slimmer than he'd seen her yet. Not that Gracie was fat, but he wouldn't call her scrawny, either.

"Sorry I'm late," she said as she reached him. "I had to take care of some business."

"No problem." He rose and walked with her toward one of the red vinyl booths near the back. He could feel every eye in the place on them, from the bartender's to each of the old men who'd stopped in the middle of their domino game to stare at them.

"Is it me or you?" Max gestured at the men as they sat down across from each other.

Gracie glanced around the room and smiled. "Don't let them bother you. Not much new happens in Hell."

"I'd gotten that impression. Doesn't it ever get to you?"

"Not really. It's kind of—" She hesitated, then finished, "reassuring. Besides, my job brings a few surprises now and then." Her eyes clouded, her expression became solemn.

"Not all good ones, I take it?"

"Not hardly. About a year ago, a man came through the county on a crime spree. Killed three people before we could apprehend him. Surprises like that I can do without."

Max had read about the case when it happened, but he hadn't connected it with Gracie until she mentioned it. "I remember reading about that. The papers called you a heroine."

She snorted. "Nothing heroic about it. Just doing my job, same as any other cop."

If it was the case he thought it was, she'd done a damn fine job of capturing the suspect and preventing him from killing yet another victim. "That's not what the newspapers said."

She scowled. "They like to sell papers. So I guess Mr. Chapman didn't take after you with his gun today?"

A modest woman, he thought, accepting the change of subject with a smile. "No, I got to take my samples in peace."

"That's good. How long do you think you'll be around?"

"As long as it takes to get the job done. I'm not in as big a hurry as I was at first, though." He gave her a provocative smile and took her hand.

"Hell's turned out to be more interesting than I thought it would be."

She blushed. Max couldn't remember the last woman he'd seen blush—at least from that mild of an innuendo. Experimentally, he ran his thumb over her palm. Her flush deepened.

"Have you always lived here?" he asked her, beginning to really enjoy himself. Pleased at her reaction, he released her hand.

She took a sip of her drink and cleared her throat. "I grew up here, but I lived in El Paso for about seven or eight years."

"Did you like it there?"

"Sometimes." She grinned. "It had its moments, but I like it here better."

"Were you in law enforcement in El Paso?"

Nodding, she said, "A city cop. They tried me on vice for a while, but I wasn't cut out for it." Solemnly, but with her eyes dancing, she added, "Guess I didn't make a very convincing prostitute. I kept laughing at all the wrong times."

Max grinned. "That might make your clients a little suspicious." Noticing she'd finished her drink and there was no waitress in sight, he picked up their empties and went to the bar to refill them.

"Are you working tonight?" he asked when he returned, setting her drink in front of her.

"Not unless there's an emergency. Why?"

He pointed to her glass. "Lemonade?"

"Oh, that." Her finger circled the edge of the

glass, a rueful smile tilting her lips. "I don't drink. No tolerance. First time I tried it was my last. One drink and the next day I felt like I was going to die."

"A woman with no vices? You don't drink, don't cuss, don't smoke—"

"I quit smoking a couple of months ago. I still want one," she said wistfully.

"But no vices now?"

"Guess not. My daddy cured me of cussing a long time ago. When I was around ten, I came home from school with some choice words." She made a face. "To this day I can't cuss without tasting soap."

Max smiled, picturing Gracie at ten. Before he could ask another question, she asked one of her own.

"How long have you been with the EPA?"

"About six months. I worked in the private sector before that." The less time he claimed to be in, the better. He'd already noticed that Gracie's casual questions could elicit a lot of information.

"Funny," she said, gazing at him thoughtfully, "but you don't look much like an EPA agent. Or act like one, either."

Uh-oh. Better watch his step. "Why do you say that?"

"For one thing, you're a lot more talkative. The other fellas kept to themselves and didn't seem to want to know folks. You're pretty much the opposite. From what I hear, you've been talking to everyone in town."

"What can I say? I'm a friendly kind of guy." He gave her his most innocent grin. "I told you, I'm not here to investigate endangered species of insects."

"Thank the Lord for that."

Max changed the subject. "I take it from your conversation with Chapman the other day that your father was sheriff before you."

"That's right."

Her tone didn't invite further conversation, but he persevered. Though he knew the story from his earlier research, he wondered how Gracie would explain it, or if she'd even try. "So you're following in his footsteps?" He sipped his beer, waiting to see what she'd say.

"Not exactly," she answered dryly. "My father left office while under investigation for taking bribes. I don't intend for the same thing to happen to me."

Up-front and honest, he thought, admiring her. Relieved, he added another reason to the growing list of arguments why Grace O'Malley couldn't be the link in the smuggling chain. Why was he so pleased, he wondered, to be able to believe in her innocence? Simply because he liked her?

"Sorry," he said after a moment. "That must be a painful subject."

She shrugged and sipped her lemonade. "If

you stick around for long, you'll hear about it. And since my father died before being brought to trial, there's still talk about it. There are two versions. One says he's guilty and one says he isn't." Her gaze met his, her brown eyes unsmiling. "Do I need to tell you which one is the right one?"

"You don't think he was guilty."

"I know he wasn't. My father never took a bribe in his life. Someday I'm going to prove it."

Hearing the quiet confidence in her words, seeing the resolute set to her jaw, Max believed her. How long had it been since he'd believed in something—or someone—that passionately? Had he ever? Inexplicably driven to offer comfort, he covered her hand and squeezed gently. "I'm sure you will."

Her gaze lifted to his, as if she were assessing his sincerity. He held on to her hand, trying to reconcile this woman determined to clear her father's name with a woman who profited from bringing illegal aliens into the country. A woman who kept a houseful of unwanted dogs and cats with a woman who made a bundle off desperate people. A woman who put herself between a madman's gun and an innocent victim with a woman who used her office to break the law. He couldn't do it.

Okay, if Gracie was innocent, that left Dunn as the most likely suspect. Assuming, of course, that the problem lay with the sheriff's office and not within Border Patrol. If he could tell Gracie the truth about why he was there and ask for her help . . .

No, it wasn't possible. His captain would question his sanity, for one thing. Telling Gracie anything would put his job on the line. His orders specifically stated the need for confidentiality. Everyone was suspect, and he'd best not forget it. He hadn't proven that she wasn't guilty, her innocence was just his gut feeling. But Max trusted his gut.

"Max?"

Her hand fluttered in his, making him aware he still held it. He smiled and got to his feet, pulling her with him. "Come on. I asked you to shoot pool, and we haven't had a game yet."

He watched her picking out a pool cue, giving it her undivided attention. The idea of Gracie lavishing that total attention on him appealed to him a hell of a lot more than it should have. *Forget it, Max*, he told himself. *Make friends, not time.*

She turned around and bestowed a blinding smile on him. "Eight ball all right with you?"

"Fine." He felt like he'd been gut punched. A woman's smile had never done that to him before. Her smile made him think of spring—a time of hope, of new beginnings. He hadn't believed in that kind of thing for years. He was starting to think Grace O'Malley was a dangerous woman.

She chalked her cue and asked, "Do you want to break?"

"No, you go ahead."

"You're gonna regret that, sonny," an old-timer sitting at a nearby table said, his cackle resounding in the smoke-filled bar.

"Am I?" Max asked her.

No reply. This time her smile was wicked as she leaned over the table and took aim. Three balls sank with her first shot.

The old man had it right, Max thought a few minutes later. In less time than it took most people to rack the balls, Gracie ran the table. Smooth and effortless. There wasn't a damned thing he could do but stand there and watch.

"Eight ball in the corner pocket," he heard her say, and game one went down the tubes.

The next game she missed a shot, which Max suspected she did on purpose. Though a decent enough player, he was nowhere near her league. It didn't bother him. Much.

Okay, so it did. His pride sure took a beating around her. She'd arrested him, rescued him, and now she was beating the socks off him at pool, for Pete's sake. Didn't she ever lose that edge?

He remembered a time she hadn't seemed so much in charge. A couple of nights earlier at her house. She hadn't been so sure of herself then. Or tonight, either, when he'd flirted with her. The temptation to find out just how flustered he could make Grace O'Malley was becoming damned near impossible to resist.

It occurred to him one reason why he was so gung ho to believe in her innocence. If he slept

with her believing her guilty, that could compro-
mise his investigation. Guilty, she was off limits.
Innocent, though . . . That was a different matter.

Hell had possibilities he hadn't even begun to
explore. He caught her gaze and smiled, imagin-
ing what she'd do if—or when—he acted on some
of his impulses.

He was doing it again, Gracie thought. Smiling at her like she was the only woman in the
world—or the only one he wanted to be with,
anyway. How did he do that? And why, she asked
herself, did she feel so flustered around him? Max
Ridell was no different from any other man she'd
played pool with, joked with, or talked to a hundred times in the past. He was only being nice
from boredom and the fact that he figured he
needed her help if he was going to get his job
done. So why did she keep thinking that he might
have other reasons? That maybe here was a man
who saw her as a woman, and not just Sheriff
O'Malley—or worse, Gracie, everybody's friend.

A couple of hours later Gracie didn't know a
whole lot more about Max, but he sure knew a lot
about her. After a few games they abandoned the
pool table and went back to the booth and talked.
He was a good listener, almost too good. She also
decided that no matter how nice he was being to
her, to think that he meant anything by it was
about as foolish as picking a fight with a porcu-
pine.

"It's nice to know somebody around here doesn't hate my guts," he told her when they called it a night and left the pool hall.

"I thought you said you didn't have any problems today," she said as they reached the patrol car.

He leaned back against the car door, crossed his arms over his chest, and smiled at her. "Only because I didn't see Chapman. If his reaction is a sample of how the other ranchers will treat me, then you're going to be rescuing me again."

"It's my job, Max. You don't have to kiss up to me."

"Is that what you think I'm doing?"

She looked him up and down, a half-smile on her lips. "Yep." No matter how much she might wish she was wrong, she didn't think she was. And Gracie preferred truth to fantasy.

Max stepped closer to her, slid his arm around her waist, and tilted her chin up with his other hand. "What if you're wrong?"

Could she be? Gazing into his eyes, she decided he could make her believe almost anything at all.

"I'm not kissing up to you," he said, his voice washing over her like a midnight tide. "I just plain want to kiss you."

Gracie's stomach somersaulted as she stared at him, every coherent thought fleeing from her head. Moonlight chased across his face, highlighting prominent cheekbones, seductively smiling eyes, the shape of his firm, masculine mouth. He smiled again, slow and sexy, and set his mouth on hers.

There was no "just plain" about it. She'd kissed men before and what Max did with his lips and tongue didn't in any way compare. His tongue probed her mouth gently, opening her lips, inviting himself inside. Her arms crept up and wrapped around his neck as she gave herself to the myriad sensations his kiss evoked. There was wonder, that a man's mouth could be so hard, yet so incredibly soft at the same time. And desire, a lingering burn that started in her belly and spread to her arms, her legs, her breasts. And longing, to feel more, give more, explore more.

When his hand slid from her face down to her waist, then to her hips to pull her against him, she didn't resist, but melted closer still. Oh Lord, she was in serious trouble. She was even hearing bells . . . Bells?

He broke the kiss and spoke in her ear. "Your pocket is ringing."

Uncomprehending, she gazed at him. He grinned, slid her cellular phone out of her hip pocket, and handed it to her. Fumbling with it, she opened it upside down before finally righting it and holding it to her ear.

"O'Malley." This had better be good, she thought.

"Sheriff, Deputy Dunn needs you to meet him at the motel," Cheryl, the night dispatcher, said.

"Why?"

"There's a report of a dead body. He says for you to come right away."

"In one of the rooms?"

"No, by the Dumpster. That's all Leroy said."

Well, she couldn't gripe about it not being important. Gracie stabbed the fingers of her free hand through her hair. "I'm on my way." A siren wailed nearby as she closed the phone and turned to Max. "Sorry, I've got to go."

"Something serious?"

"Dead bodies are usually serious. It's over at the motel."

FIVE

"I thought it was a raccoon," Bud Bartlett said for the fifth time since Gracie had arrived at the motel. "You know how they've been hanging around my Dumpsters. How was I supposed to know? I'd 'a never shot him if I'd known. You gotta believe me, Sheriff."

"Steady there, Bud," Gracie said, patting his arm. She had warned Bud time and again about shooting at those raccoons, for fear that something like this would happen, though she hadn't expected quite such a tragedy. No point in reminding him of that, though. Nothing to be done about it now.

"Why don't you go on inside and have Ida fix you a cup of coffee? I'll be back to talk to you some more after we investigate things here." With Bud carrying on she hadn't even had a chance to look at the scene. If anybody could calm him down, his wife Ida could.

She walked over to the Dumpster where Leroy stood by the body, holding back the small crowd drawn by the ruckus. Thanks to Bud's ongoing battle with the raccoons, gunshots were a near nightly occurrence, but Leroy had used his siren when he answered the call. That had drawn a crowd in a hurry. Everyone staying at the motel was there, of course, Max included. He had followed her from the pool hall and now stood on the edge of the group of people.

Leroy was trying, with no success, to get folks to leave, but Gracie didn't waste her energy on impossible tasks. As long as they didn't get close enough to obscure the scene, she figured that was the best she could hope for.

"Fill me in," she told her deputy when she reached him.

Checking his watch, Leroy said, "Dispatch notified me about fifteen minutes ago. Coroner's on his way. Ida called it in as soon as they realized it was a man. He was already dead, she said. Think it's one of them illegals, Sheriff?"

It seemed likely, Gracie thought, though she gave no voice to her opinion. Looking down at the crumpled body lying on its back in the shadows, she could hardly imagine the hunger that had driven the victim. Who else but an illegal immigrant would be nosing around a Dumpster? Hell didn't have any homeless, not unless you counted illegals passing through. So many of them were desperately needy. Hunger wasn't just a word to them—it was a way of life. Which was one reason they risked what they did to cross over to the U.S.

"Shine that light down there so I can see," she said to Leroy. "I don't have mine with me." Curbing her irritation, she wondered if he held the light poorly just to annoy her. "Never mind," she said, exasperated as he played it everywhere but where she needed it. "Let me borrow it for a while."

Once she got past the bloody chest to the deceased's face, she was surprised to see clearly Asian features rather than the Hispanic ones she'd expected. "Well, lookee here," she said, more to herself than her deputy.

"Look at what, Sheriff?"

Glancing at the deputy, she gestured at the dead man. "Notice anything unusual?"

Leroy nudged the body with the toe of his boot. "He's no Mexican, if that's what you mean," he said impatiently. "Chinese, I guess. But he's still an illegal."

"Most likely." Kneeling down, she methodically went through the dead man's pockets while the deputy waited with growing restlessness. Nothing, she thought. Not a blessed scrap. "No papers, no identification, not even a wallet," she said. "I'd say you're right, Leroy."

The deputy made a sound of satisfaction.

"Alert Border Patrol. They'll want to know

about this right away." Border Patrol had been investigating a rash of immigrants coming from China and Pakistan, smuggled in through Mexico. Looked like there was another case for them.

Rising, she aimed the light at the surrounding dirt. She saw boot prints, and a couple of other prints, but she didn't see prints from a huarache sole. The dead man wore huaraches. Unless he'd flown, he hadn't gotten to the Dumpster under his own power. A Chinese immigrant wearing huaraches. Weirder and weirder, she thought.

"Make sure you keep those folks away from the crime scene," she told the deputy. "We don't need any more prints than are already here. And call in some help. We're going to need it."

"What do we need more help for? Sheriff, what are you doing?" he called after her as she wandered down the dirt alleyway. "It's cut-and-dried, what happened."

No, it wasn't. But Leroy had a bad habit of never looking further than what was right in front of his face. Gracie tried not to be too hard on him because he did have his good points. He'd been her father's deputy—his protégé who had assumed more and more responsibilities as Mike O'Malley's illness had taken its toll. But more than that, Leroy had stuck by him when others insisted Sheriff Mike O'Malley was crooked. That was something Gracie would never forget.

Still, try as she might, she couldn't like him. Leroy had been interim sheriff, and surprisingly, hadn't run against her. But Gracie knew he didn't like her authority over him, nor did she really understand why he remained her deputy. Especially when she suspected Leroy didn't like her any better than she liked him.

"Need some help?" Max asked.

She stood at the entrance to the dirt alley, a couple hundred yards away from the Dumpster. "Not unless you know of a way to get those folks to go on about their business. You're not supposed to be here, either, you know."

He grinned and held up a high-powered flashlight. "Deputy Dog has his hands full over there." He motioned toward the Dumpster. "Thought you could use some more light."

In spite of the situation, she smiled at his name for Leroy, not denying the light would be welcome. "Thanks."

"Glad to help."

She nodded and studied the ground. If what she suspected was true, they would have parked there, close to the entrance where no one was likely to see them. The motel was the third building into the alley, the first two being a laundry and a dry goods store, both closed for the evening.

"Drag marks," Max said, playing his light over the beginning of a trail.

"That's what it looks like," Gracie said, studying them. It took a minute for his words to penetrate. She raised her eyes and stared at him.

He was gazing at the crowd of people, looking

thoughtful. "They dragged the body from here to the Dumpster, I'll bet."

"And just how did you figure that out?"

He glanced at her and grinned. "It's not hard. I read a lot of detective novels. Police procedurals, true crime, things like that."

"Novels, huh?" That made sense, she supposed, although he'd sure figured it out quickly enough. But she didn't have time to puzzle out what was bothering her about his comment. Someone had to make sure no cars entered the unpaved alley. Luckily, there was only the one access. "Can you do something else for me? Until I can get some more men out here, I need to make sure no one drives down the alley."

"No problem."

"I'll send a man to relieve you as soon as somebody shows up." She walked off a few feet, then stopped and turned back to him. "Thanks. I appreciate the help."

"Anytime," Max said, flashing her a devilish smile that made her wish she wasn't in the middle of investigating a crime scene. She was the sheriff, though, and her responsibilities couldn't wait.

Max debated putting off calling his captain when he returned to his room at 2:00 A.M., but he decided the news of a dead Chinese illegal immigrant was a development his superior would want to know about no matter the hour.

After giving a thumbnail sketch of events, Max asked, "Have we found anything out about Border Patrol? Are they cleared yet?"

"No, not yet," Lloyd Towers said. "But they're not looking likely. Nothing as promising as what you've just told me. The dead man being Chinese supports the theory that the smugglers are increasing the load of Asians, since they can get better prices for bringing them in."

Promising, Max thought. Tell that to the poor sucker who had died that evening. But he knew what the captain meant. The Chinese and Pakistani were so eager to immigrate, they were rumored to pay as much as forty thousand dollars a head. Add to that the price of the drugs that came in with nearly every load and you were talking serious money.

"How did you manage to be there?" Towers continued.

"Luck. The whole thing took place at my motel. They set it up to look like the motel owner killed him accidentally, but we—the sheriff, that is—found evidence of the body being dragged down the alley. I heard her telling the coroner to check the spread of the shot because she didn't think the fatal shot had come from the motel owner's gun."

"The sheriff sounds bright enough from what you've told me."

"Definitely bright," Max agreed. Gracie hadn't spent five minutes with the body before she was searching the alley. He didn't think it was luck, either. She'd known what she was looking for, he'd bet on it. For a slow-moving woman she sure thought fast.

"Do you think she's involved?"

"If she wanted to she could run the whole smuggling ring, but I don't think she's the one we're after." Max thought about that evening, about all the things he'd found out about Grace O'Malley so far. None of it added up to the mastermind of a smuggling scheme, or a participant, either, as far as he was concerned. "No. I'm nearly positive she isn't involved, but her deputy's another matter."

"So you're liking the deputy for it?"

"He's got a brand-new, kick-ass truck that cost him a wad. Don't know what else he's got, but he's rumored to have come into an inheritance. Distant relative supposedly left it to him." He had diner gossip to thank for that information. "The sheriff drives a twenty-year-old pickup that sounds like it hasn't had a tune-up in almost that long. I've seen her place too. If she's got money she's hiding it well."

"Women are good at hiding things," Towers said cynically. "Don't forget that when you're concentrating so hard on the deputy."

Late the next afternoon Max went out to Gracie's place, intending to find out more about the incident the night before. All he'd gotten for his pains from searching another ranch that day was a warning blast from a shotgun. Damned if it hadn't almost hit its mark too. The ranchers around there were too quick on the trigger to suit Max.

The patrol car and Gracie's ancient pickup truck sat in the gravel drive next to her old-fashioned farmhouse, so he knew she was around somewhere. He didn't run her to earth either at the house or the barn, though. Maybe she was taking a walk, he thought, although the idea of voluntarily strolling in the mid-July heat boggled his mind. He was a lot more accustomed to humid north Texas heat than the dry desert heat around there, but he didn't enjoy walking in it, either.

After an initial frenzy of greeting, the dogs and cats lolled about, either in the barn, under the porch, or in whatever shade they could scare up. Max sat on the porch steps to wait for Gracie, idly rubbing the spaniel mix's head. Izzy, he remembered Gracie calling her. He liked dogs, though he hadn't had one since he was a kid. He'd forgotten how soothing petting a dog could be.

And after the night he'd had, he needed soothing. Max had been forced to take a hard look at his motivation for believing Gracie innocent. The captain was right, he admitted, and if he hadn't been so busy thinking with his zipper instead of his head, he'd have remembered that.

Tower's words had echoed in his mind for half the night. "Women are good at hiding things," he'd said. God, that was a statement of fact if he'd ever heard one. His wife had been great at telling him one thing, all the while having a hidden agenda. It wasn't too difficult to imagine that Gracie might have one too. Just because she *seemed* open and aboveboard didn't mean she actually was.

About ten minutes later, Gracie came around the side of the house with a shovel slung over one shoulder. For a moment she checked, looked right at him, then continued walking toward the barn as if he weren't there.

What the devil was the matter with her? He rose to follow her. "Gracie?"

"Go away, Max," she said, not turning around. "I'm not much in the mood for company."

He caught up to her at the barn entrance, laying a hand on her arm to stop her. When she looked at him he noticed with surprise her tear-stained cheeks. It clicked as he saw the mud clinging to the shovel and ground into the knees of her khaki slacks. "Did one of your animals die?"

"No." She jerked out of his grasp, opened a door to what looked like a tack room, and stepped inside. "Can we talk later? Unless this is really important—"

"What's wrong? What are you so upset about?"

"I'm not upset." She slapped the shovel against the wall, catching it on the hooks that held it to a Peg-Board.

"You're giving a good imitation of it."

She slammed her fist against the Peg-Board so hard, he was surprised the shovel didn't fall off. "I'm not upset. I'm mad." Spinning around, she glared at him and said flatly, "They killed that poor dog just to get to me."

And succeeded, Max thought, though still mystified. He hadn't imagined Gracie could get this agitated about anything. "What happened?"

Putting her hands to her temples, she closed her eyes, unmindful of the mud now liberally streaking her face. "A week or so ago I busted some folks for dogfighting. We've been going round and round about it for months." She dropped her hands and looked at him, anger darkening her eyes until they appeared nearly black. "This afternoon when I left the jail, somebody had left a present on the hood of my patrol car. I just got finished burying him."

Her tears were for an animal she hadn't even known. How could anyone so softhearted be a successful cop—or run a human smuggling ring, for that matter? His belief in her possible guilt took another nosedive. "You brought it home?"

"Well, I suppose I could've thrown him in the Dumpster like Leroy thought I should," she said with a bitter drawl, "but it seemed like the least I could do was bury him. Especially since they wouldn't have killed him except to get to me." She stalked out of the tiny room and flung over her shoulder, "And don't tell me I'm bound to have seen worse things. Leroy's already reminded me of that too."

"I hope to God I never say the same thing Deputy Dog does," Max muttered, and followed her. When he walked into the kitchen, he found her at the sink washing her hands.

"Why are you still around?" she asked, giving him a sharp glance. "Here I am, yelling at you about something that's no fault of yours and you hang around waiting for more?"

Max folded his arms over his chest and watched her. If she wasn't careful, she'd scrub the skin right off her hands. He lifted one shoulder in a shrug. "Call me a masochist."

For a moment she didn't speak. When she did, her voice was low and strained, so low, he almost couldn't hear it above the running water. "I'm sorry."

He stepped closer to her and picked up the dish towel on the drain board, running a corner of it under the warm water. Turning her face up with one hand, he wiped away the mud and tear streaks, pushing her straight dark red-brown hair back from her brow as he did so. Her eyes still crackled with anger, but they held a deeper, sadder look as well. What would it be like, he wondered, to feel things as Gracie did? To feel so strongly, so passionately? So compassionately.

"No apologies necessary. You needed to vent." He shut off the water, dried her hands on the dish towel.

As soon as he'd finished, she pulled away and walked into the living room. Max followed, standing beside the comfortable, overstuffed sofa and watching her pace the room.

"That little dog was just a throwaway," she said over her shoulder. "Nameless, homeless, worthless. Nobody cares that dog died."

Her voice was hoarse—from tears or anger, he wasn't sure which. "Nobody except you."

Her pacing stopped a moment, her gaze meeting his. "That's the problem. They know my weakness."

Since he didn't have an answer to that, he said nothing. She was exactly right, cops couldn't afford a weakness of that kind. Maybe that was why some of the best cops he knew seemed like heartless bastards most of the time. Max knew from experience, if you let things get to you too much, you couldn't deal with the ugliness. Of course, they paid a price for it—in high divorce rates, alcoholism, ill health.

Gracie threw herself down on the couch, rubbing her temples before she spoke. "It's just like that man we found last night. He was a throwaway too. Nobody would've cared about him, either. Except for one thing."

So the dog wasn't the only thing bothering her. He'd wondered what she'd thought about the previous night. She'd hidden her emotions well. "What thing is that?"

"He was Chinese. Nobody would have given a flip if he was Mexican."

A part of him didn't want to pump her, but he had a job to do. He took a seat beside her and said, "I don't understand. What does his nationality have to do with anything?"

"Chinese and Pakistanis pay ten times the price to get into the States as Mexican illegals do. Border Patrol's tracking a smuggling ring they believe is bringing them through the Texas-Mexican border. This could be a big break in their case. They don't care that he was a man, just like them, with family, friends. Or that somebody took him out and shot him down, then dumped him in the trash. Or that whoever killed him tried to frame an innocent man. Can you imagine what Bud must have felt, thinking he killed a man?"

Max raised a hand to her face, cupping her cheek. "But you care, don't you?"

Impatiently, she jerked her head away. "Of course I care. It happened in my county. It's my responsibility to investigate the crime."

"It's more than just the job, though, isn't it?" Touching her arm, he rubbed it comfortingly.

"Maybe. It's just . . ." She sighed and shrugged helplessly. "Some of these folks are so desperate to leave their homes, they're willing to put up with anything, do anything, to even have a chance at getting into the States. It's hard to imagine the kind of life they're fleeing."

Were Gracie's sympathies so strong, she'd be

willing to look the other way while these people made a bid at a better life? Max wondered uneasily. That was something he could imagine, unlike her doing it for profit. And dammit, he didn't want to imagine it. He didn't want the captain to be right. Not about Gracie. He wanted her to be exactly what she seemed to be. A loving, generous, caring woman. An honest woman.

"Sometimes," she said, "I just want to forget about the things I have to do, the things I see, but . . . I can't."

He wanted to make her feel better. Wanted to offer comfort, sympathy, but he didn't know how. Forgetting, though—he was good at that. His gaze dropped to her mouth, to her tempting lips, trembling in invitation. "If forgetting is what you're after," he said, lowering his voice, "I think I can help you out."

Her gaze widened, linked with his. A pulse beat at the hollow of her throat where her khaki shirt was unbuttoned. "How?" It came out a whisper.

Smiling, he watched her moisten her lips as her breath came faster. He cupped her chin, slid his hand down the smooth skin of her neck and up again. A kiss or two, nothing more, he thought. He tilted her head back and bent his own to taste her. Sweet. Salty. Sexy. His tongue traced the seam of her lips until they parted. She accepted his tongue, drawing it in and meeting it with darting thrusts of her own.

A kiss of comfort, he'd believed. But it wasn't. Once his mouth touched hers, he wanted more, and he knew by the moan deep in her throat, by the answering quest of her tongue, by the softening of her lips under his, that she did too.

Indulging them both, he put his arms around her, pulled her closer, and took the kiss another level deeper. Her arms twined around his neck, and her fingers dived into his hair. Her breasts pressed against him as the heat between them blazed, and Max forgot about everything but the woman in his arms and easing the suddenly raging ache in his loins.

Leaning her back against the couch cushions, he trailed his lips along her jaw, down her neck, to the hollow of her throat. Her pulse beat rapidly, fluttering in wild beats against his open mouth. His hand teased her breast, her nipple beading in response. He tugged at it with his fingers, smiling when she moaned again, arched her back, and pressed her breast upward.

He returned to her mouth, taking his time to explore every seductive part of it, tasting, touching, reveling in her reaction. Gracie was an odd combination of shyness and boldness, one moment holding back and the next answering him with a tempting dance of her tongue against his. He drew back, reaching for the buttons of her shirt, waiting for her to stop him, but she made no move to do so.

Her eyes wide and dazed already with passion,

she gazed at him. Her hands clutched at his shoulders, her chest rose and fell quickly, her lips gleamed, red and plump from his kisses. The buttons came undone easily, and he opened her shirt to expose a plain, no-nonsense white cotton bra. Utilitarian, not provocative, it made him smile and turned him on at the same time. The smoky look in her eyes notched the heat up even higher. His gaze dropped to her chest again. He could see her nipples peaking, enticing him, and bent to suckle one through the fabric.

Gracie gasped, her hands tightening before moving to hold his head against her breast. They sank deeper into the couch, her legs parting so he could settle between them. He felt her body's welcome, her softness to his hardness. He pulled her bra straps down until they caught in her blouse, and tormented first one bare breast then the other. He wanted her, needed her, needed the hot give-and-take of sex. And her taste taunted his senses until he was filled with it.

Her body had surrendered so sweetly, melting with his kisses, burning with response to each lingering caress. He raised his head and looked at her, at her head thrown back in abandon, the inviting gleam of her creamy skin, and in that instant sanity returned. What the hell was he doing?

He was supposed to be offering comfort, not seducing her. It wasn't fair, or right, to make love to her now. He knew it, even if she didn't. "We'd better . . ." He hesitated, the sight of her swollen lips and flushed cheeks tempting him to say the hell with it and continue what he'd started. "Dammit, I can't do this."

Her eyes widened, and he saw the hurt flash in them. Poor choice of words, he thought. He shoved himself off her, got up, and turned his back, giving her a chance to straighten her clothes. "What I meant is, we shouldn't—I shouldn't have let things go so far."

"Why?" She'd pulled her blouse together over her breasts and was sitting up looking at him.

Ill at ease, he stuffed his hands in his pockets and paced away a step. "Look, Gracie, I'm only going to be in town until my job is finished." His real job, not the fake one. "It wouldn't be fair to you to . . ." He allowed his voice to trail off, not wanting to spell it out for her.

She'd finished buttoning her blouse. Her face had that blank look, the one that had made him wonder when he first met her if she wasn't a little dense. Now that he'd gotten to know her, he realized there was a whole lot going on behind that expressionless gaze. But he didn't have a clue what she was thinking at that moment.

He waited for her to speak but she didn't. She simply stood, still looking at him. "Well, I—I guess I'd better get going," he finally said, breaking the awkward silence.

"Yeah, I guess you'd better."

Reluctantly, he started for the door, pausing when he got there to look at her over his shoulder. Dammit, he didn't want to leave her, not like this. But if he stayed he'd make love to her and he didn't think either of them was ready to deal with all the ramifications of that.

He'd done the right thing, not making love to her. So why did he feel like a total slime?

SIX

She was no good at men, Gracie thought after Max left. Never had been. The past few minutes proved she hadn't changed lately either.

That wasn't altogether true, though. Men as friends weren't a problem, it was the romantic aspects she just didn't get. She understood men pretty well, or so she'd thought. You couldn't be a cop as long as she had and not have a decent idea of what makes men tick.

But she didn't understand Max at all.

Connie might be able to help her, Gracie thought. Come to think of it, with an ex-husband, a fiancé, and Lord only knew how many men in her past, Connie would be the perfect person to talk to.

Or would she? Gracie asked herself as she got in her truck to drive to Connie's house. Her friend didn't always have the best judgment when it came to men. And what if she was involved with Leroy Dunn, like Max had hinted the other day? Had Connie started something with Leroy because she was unhappy with Reese? Gracie knew they'd been having problems, but she hadn't thought they were that serious. Not enough for Connie to take up with another man.

When she turned the key she heard an ominous clicking and groaned. Dadgummit, the truck needed a trip to the repair shop, but the only mechanic in town was Jim Bob Mulligan. Considering Jim Bob hated her guts, she'd no more trust him with a vehicle of hers than she'd trust a rabbit with a truck full of lettuce. She got out, raised the hood, and fiddled with the battery cables.

Crossing her fingers, she got back in and turned the key again. The engine sputtered to life and caught. She didn't put the truck in gear yet, though, trying to decide whether to go to her friend or not. But who else could she turn to? Since her father had died, just a few short years after Gracie's mother, Connie was as close to family as Gracie had. Connie knew her better than anybody else.

She could hang around home, driving herself cuckoo trying to figure out that blasted man or she could go to Connie's. No contest, she decided, and headed out.

The house was dark when she arrived. Gracie's hopes dwindled, but Connie answered when she rang the bell, asking who was there through the closed door. Glad to see her friend finally heeding some of her advice, Gracie said, "It's me. I need to talk to you."

"Gracie? What are you doing here? I didn't— we weren't supposed to do something, were we?"

She sounded shocked. Almost panicky, if Gracie were the fanciful type. "No, I just dropped by. Open up, Con."

Gracie heard her fumbling with the lock before the door finally swung open. Stepping inside, she walked toward the couch and said, "Why are you sitting around in the dark? I thought you weren't here. Let me turn on some—"

"No, don't!" Connie said, intercepting Gracie's hand before she could flick on the lamp. "I've got a headache."

"One of your migraines?" Gracie asked sympathetically. Although she got bad headaches herself, they weren't like the killer ones her friend suffered from. "I'm sorry. We can talk another time."

"No, that's all right." Connie muted the TV, the only source of light, and sat on the couch. "What's going on? I thought you were working?"

"Not tonight. Leroy's got it." Taking a seat beside her, Gracie wondered what was going on. Usually when her friend had one of her sick headaches, she took to bed in a darkened room and you couldn't get her up until it passed. "Is something wrong? Besides your headache?"

Head averted, Connie didn't answer. Gracie

realized she'd yet to look her in the face and wondered why. More patient than Connie ever would be, she simply waited.

Finally, Connie sighed, a sound of frustration. "Might as well tell you, I guess. Everybody in town will know by tomorrow anyway, when I go to work." She reached behind her and flicked the lamp on.

When Connie turned toward her, Gracie couldn't stop a horrified gasp. Connie's right eye had swollen nearly shut, her cheek and the right side of her mouth were bruised and puffy. Her lip was split. She looked like the loser in a bout with Mike Tyson.

"Sweet Lord," Gracie whispered. Her hand went out to touch her friend's cheek, dropping when Connie flinched and jerked her head away. "What happened? Did Reese—?"

"No, Reese didn't," Connie said tartly. "I knew you'd think that. Once a cop, always a cop."

Gracie didn't believe that Reese, who was one of the least violent men she knew, would ever lay a hand on a woman, but Connie sure looked like someone had used her as a punching bag. And if it wasn't Reese, then who was it?

Oh, Lord, was it Leroy? Had Connie really taken up with Leroy Dunn? He was a bully, Gracie knew. She'd seen it and called him on it more than a time or two in the past eighteen months. It didn't take a speck of imagination for her to picture him slapping a woman around, especially if she'd been giving him lip. When she had a mind to be, Connie was mouthy as the dickens.

And Reese was right-handed. Connie's bruises were more consistent with a left-handed batterer. Left-handed. Like Leroy Dunn. Her stomach heaved with anger and nausea.

"Well, what happened then?" she asked, masking her anger, trying to sound reasonable.

"I ran into a door." Connie's voice was flat, emotionless.

Gracie simply looked at her, unwilling to call her a liar.

"I know you don't believe me, but that's what happened."

"Talk to me, Con. Either as your friend or as the sheriff, but please don't shut me out."

"I'm telling you," she said, her voice rising, "I ran into a door. Reese and I had another fight last night, so I got drunk and this"—she pointed to her cheek—"is what happened."

Though she didn't believe her for a minute, Gracie knew there was nothing she could do if Connie wouldn't trust her and talk to her. But it hurt, both as a friend and as a law officer, not to be able to help her.

Touching Connie's knee, she said, "If you decide to talk about it, or to bring charges, I'm here. I won't nag you. It's your decision." She wanted to nag her, though, and would have if she believed it would do any good.

For a moment she thought Connie might start

to talk, but the other woman only said, "Tell me why you came over."

Curbing her frustration, Gracie answered. "It's not important. We can talk some other time." How could she talk to Connie now? Especially now?

"You came over for a reason. You said you wanted to talk. Go ahead and tell me, dammit."

Maybe telling Connie her own problem would get her to open up. She sure wasn't talking now. What did she have to lose? Then Gracie realized she had no earthly idea how to start the conversation. Explain men to me? Explain Max to me? Tell me why he—

"Is it Max?"

Startled, she stared at Connie. "How did you know?"

"You've got that goofy look on your face again. You get it every time you talk about him. Or think about him, I'll bet."

Gracie didn't deny it. Connie was probably right. "He came over tonight."

"And?"

"Darn it, Con, I don't understand him at all!" Gracie burst out. "One minute he acts like he likes me and then he just—leaves."

"Define acting like he likes you."

Kissing the fire out of her, for one thing, she thought, and blushed.

"Oh, my God, you slept with him."

"No, I didn't. But I would have. Except he just up and left."

Goggling at her like that, Connie looked exactly like a pollywog, Gracie thought irritably.

"Right in the middle of—"

"He said he shouldn't have kissed me like he had and something about not being fair to me. Then he left."

"Did he know you were willing? Maybe he thinks you're not."

Gracie laughed shortly. "Oh, I think he's got a pretty good idea of what I'm willing to do," she said, remembering her response to his kisses. He'd gotten her all heated up, which he couldn't have helped but know, and then walked out the door. He didn't want her, that was the problem.

"Hmm," Connie said, in her let-me-think-about-this tone. "Why wouldn't it be fair to you?"

"Because he's leaving town after his job's finished. Have you ever heard of anything so dumb?" Boy howdy, that was a lame excuse if Gracie had ever heard one.

Narrowing her eyes, Connie nodded and tapped her finger against her leg. "He's being noble," she announced after a moment, as though she'd just made a great discovery.

"Noble? What the heck does that mean?" Frustrated, she frowned at her friend.

"Honey, it's obvious you're not a fling-type woman. Max has told you he's not sticking around. Maybe he's afraid you'll get hurt, that you don't understand the rules."

"Rules?" Gracie flung a hand up in a rare gesture of frustration. "Since when do men care about that? From what I've heard—and don't forget, I've heard a lot of guys talk—most men just want to get a woman into bed. They're not that picky how they accomplish it, either, as long as they get them there." She shook her head. "Admit it. You've said the same thing often enough. No, the problem is, he's not attracted to me." Just like other men. And she'd thought Max was different. Thought he saw her as a woman. Well, she'd been wrong.

"He kissed you, didn't he?"

Brother, had he. "Yeah, but one minute he's kissing me like there's no tomorrow, and the next he's backing out the door so fast, my head started spinning like Linda Blair's in *The Exorcist*."

Connie's grin was a bit lopsided, like it hurt her to smile. "Sounds like a major attack of nobility to me. What do you want, Gracie?"

What did she want? She wanted Max. For the first time in her life, she wanted to go to bed with a man. Not just any man, but Max Ridell. Her lips curved into a smile when she thought about him, about making love with him. Though she was a little hazy on the details, she knew it would be wonderful.

Could Connie be right? Had he stopped because he didn't want her to get hurt? What would it feel like to have his hands on her, and hers on him? To feel his mouth tasting her skin like he'd done earlier that night, but not stopping when, or where, he had. She flushed, wishing she didn't have such a great imagination.

"You've got it bad, girlfriend," Connie said. "It just so happens, I've got the perfect solution."

"What?" she asked suspiciously.

"Simple. Seduce him."

Gracie laughed, halting abruptly when she realized Connie was serious. "Seduce him? I couldn't seduce that lamp. Wouldn't even know how to start."

"Honey child, take it from me, a man's a lot easier to seduce than a lamp."

"What the hell?" Seven A.M. was too early, Max thought, to have your day start tubing down the drain. Four flat tires were hard to ignore, though. Squatting, he examined one of them. Slashed. Somebody wasn't happy with him. Or maybe somebody didn't want him to do any work that day.

Back in his room, he called the sheriff's office to report the vandalism and find out where he could get new tires. Somehow he didn't think Hell would have what he needed.

"O'Malley."

The sound of her voice did odd things to his

gut. He didn't like it, especially since he'd burned all his bridges with her the night before. Which, he admitted, had been a stupid thing to do. He should have at least strung her along, used his friendship with her to help him find out more about the smuggling ring. Instead, he'd had an attack of conscience and blown the whole deal.

"It's Max, Gracie." She didn't speak. "My truck was vandalized last night. Tires slashed."

"Any idea who did it?"

She sounded professional. All business. He missed the husky drawl.

"Somebody who doesn't like the EPA, I'd guess." Which gave her a boatload of suspects.

"Be there as soon as I can. Don't touch anything, just in case they were careless enough to leave prints."

"Do you know where I can get new tires? I can't get any work done with no wheels."

"Oh, that's right. You're wanting to finish up as fast as you can, aren't you? Do the job and hit the road, huh?"

"Gracie, I—"

"Mulligan's Mechanics."

"Mulligan? As in Jim Bob?"

"Yep. That's him," she said, laughter in her voice. "See you in a little bit."

Great. He'd be lucky if he got the tires by Christmas.

Half an hour later, her pen poised over a crime

report attached to a clipboard, Gracie asked him, "Anything else?"

Dressed in her khaki uniform, with her white cowboy hat, her badge and gun belt, Gracie looked like she had the first time he met her. Except this time she was more impersonal. Like they hadn't exchanged first names, much less a kiss that had made him ache for hours afterward. She was acting like she hardly knew him, he thought, illogically irritated. What did he expect after the way he'd left her the night before?

Stuffing his hands in his pockets, he frowned and shook his head. "Nothing. You'd think I'd have heard something."

"Why would you have? Are you that light of a sleeper?"

"Sometimes. Especially on nights when I'm not sleeping well anyway." That brought her gaze up to meet his. "Gracie, about what I said last night—"

"I don't think we need to talk about that. You made yourself clear enough then."

Damn, damn, damn. She didn't sound angry but she was bound to be. When was he going to learn that doing the right thing nearly always backfired? You'd think his marriage would have taught him that lesson.

"The last thing I meant to do—"

"Forget about it, Max. No hard feelings, okay?"

Right. Now why didn't he trust her?

"You don't look like you believe me," she said, a smile tugging at her mouth. "Look, I thought about it and you're right. I was upset last night. If we'd—" She hesitated and shrugged. "It would have been a mistake. So I'm grateful to you."

A mistake? It would have been great, he thought, anger licking an irrational flame. She was grateful to him. Grateful that they hadn't made love. If that wasn't the *damnedest* thing he'd ever heard.

"Is Jim Bob ordering the tires for you?"

"Yeah." He gave a bark of unamused laughter. "For double the going rate."

She nodded. "At least he's doing it. If he didn't want money more than revenge, you'd be in big trouble. Tell you what, you can borrow my pickup. I'm working anyway, so I won't need it. Come on, I'll take you to get it." She turned and started walking to the patrol car.

My God, she meant it, he thought, staring after her. Just like that, they were friends again. She was amazing. He couldn't think of a single other woman who'd have done the same thing.

Grace O'Malley, the most generous, warmhearted woman he'd ever known. She was a threat. To his peace of mind. To the lessons he'd learned about women from his miserable marriage and his subsequent affairs.

He'd be crazy to get involved with Gracie. One more time, he reminded himself he was in

Hell to break a smuggling ring. Seducing the town's sheriff had no place in his plans.

So why couldn't he keep his mind on the smuggling and off the image of Gracie in bed with him?

SEVEN

Two days later, Max had revised his opinion about Gracie's generosity. Now he knew that she'd lent him that thing she called a truck as payback. Ringing her doorbell, he thanked God his own truck was supposed to be ready the next day. Who cared if it cost him two weeks' salary to get it back?

"What's wrong?" she asked when she opened the kitchen door and saw him.

Max stalked inside, tossed her key on the counter, and turned to glare at her. "Why don't you just shoot the damn thing and put it out of its misery?"

She stared at him, her coffee-colored eyes looking mystified. "What?"

"Your truck." He snarled the words rather than spoke them.

Her mouth quirked. "Guess it died on you, huh?"

"Yeah, I guess it did," he said, matching his drawl to hers.

"Now wait just a cotton-pickin' minute." She propped her hands on her hips and gave him back glare for glare. "You were happy enough to borrow it a couple of days ago."

"That was before it died on me in one-hundred-and-ten-degree heat with a pack of dogs circling me, out for blood. My blood."

"Dog pack? Wild dogs?" Her tone sharpened, and she sounded like the sheriff now.

Max shook his head. "It wasn't exactly a pack. There were two of them."

"Still, if there are wild dogs loose, I'd better send my deputy to check it out."

"They're long gone by now, and I don't think they were wild. Never mind." Closing his eyes, he leaned his head back, rubbed his neck, and groaned. "What I'd give for a cold beer," he muttered.

"I don't have a beer, but I can give you a glass of wine."

"Sold," he said, and opened his eyes. "Thanks."

Okay, so she was right, he thought, watching her pull the wine bottle from the refrigerator. She'd lent him her pickup, miserable excuse for a vehicle that it was, and he had no room to gripe.

"Why don't I open it?" he asked, noticing that she didn't seem to have a glimmer of how to go about it.

"Good idea," she said, grinning and handing over the bottle and the corkscrew.

When she gave him a crystal water goblet he laughed. "Do I look like I need it that badly?"

A shy smile tugged at her mouth. "That's the closest I can get to a wineglass. But I have to say, you looked pretty riled up when you walked in. Want to tell me what happened?"

Leaning back against the counter, Max took a deep drink of the wine. Not bad. Maybe after half a bottle he wouldn't be in such a surly mood. "When I finished at the Chapmans' this afternoon, the truck wouldn't start. I was under the hood trying to fix it and next thing I knew, a couple of dogs were after me like I was dinner. I'd still be stuck in the truck if I hadn't remembered I'd put my gun in the glove compartment."

"You shot the dogs?" Her voice rose with the question.

She looked horrified. Also different, but he hadn't figured out why yet. "No, I didn't shoot the damn dogs," he said irritably. "Not that they didn't deserve it. They'd have eaten me with no compunction. I shot into the air, and they ran off. I figure Chapman set them on me, him being so fond of me."

"That's funny." Frowning, she leaned against the counter. "I've never known the Chapmans' dogs to be vicious."

"Take it from me, these were not friendly animals." Gracie was wearing a skirt, that's what was different. A short denim skirt. Extremely short. This was the first time he'd seen her legs bare. He wondered why in the hell she covered them up all the time. On second thought, maybe it was a good thing that she did.

"What kind were they?" she asked.

Long and tempting, he thought, before he realized she was talking about dogs. "The kind with big teeth," he said, his gaze leaving her legs to take a good look at the rest of her. The white scoop-necked blouse she wore emphasized her cleavage. He hadn't seen that before either. He gulped more wine and hoped he wasn't drooling.

"Ha-ha. I'm serious. What breed were they?"

Max gave himself a mental shake, but he didn't quit looking at her. "How the hell should I know? I didn't stop for introductions. I was too busy hauling my butt into the truck before they ate me alive. They were big, brown, and mean."

"Rottweilers? Dobermans?"

"Maybe Dobermans." His eyes narrowed. "Why? Where are you headed with this, Gracie?"

She folded her arms underneath her chest, which did amazing things to her breasts and nearly gave him a heart attack. With an effort he dragged his mind back to what she was saying.

"The Chapmans don't have Dobermans." Their eyes met. "In fact, I can only think of one person around here who does. And he doesn't live on the river."

"Who?"

"Leroy Dunn."

His mind returned to business with a bang, his instincts quivering like a racehorse at the starting gate. "Why would your deputy set his dogs on me?"

"Beats the heck out of me." She turned away to open the oven door. "But I aim to find out."

Did Dunn suspect he was more than an EPA agent? Max wondered. Or did he just not want anybody nosing around the Chapmans' land?

He must be closer to finding incriminating evidence than he'd believed. If Dunn had set his own dogs on him, then there was definitely something worth hiding on the Chapmans' ranch. And if his instincts were on target, Dunn was the one hiding that something.

Tantalizing smells drifted to his nostrils. He didn't mind begging for a good cause. And speaking of tantalizing, the sight of Gracie bending over in that short skirt, peering into the oven, was enough to make him seriously reconsider the decision he'd made the other night.

Then it hit him. Gracie had a date. Cooking, wearing a skirt, the wine. Hell yes, she had a date. And it wasn't with him. Which, however irrational, ticked him off royally.

"Thanks for letting me use your truck," he said abruptly. "Looks like I'd better get going." Not being able to follow up on his suspicions about Dunn lent his voice that sharp edge, he told himself. Not jealousy. If he'd known she was busy he would have stayed at the motel after his shower and waited until morning to return the damned truck.

Gracie set a casserole dish on top of the stove and waved a hot pad over it. Max's stomach rumbled as the succulent aroma drifted to him again. He told himself it was hunger that made his jaw clench and his temper spike. Any man would be irritated, being teased with luscious food. And luscious skin.

"Are you hungry?" she asked. "There's plenty for both of us, if you'd like to stay."

He raised an eyebrow in surprise. "I thought you . . ." He grinned as relief swept through him, totally out of proportion to what he should have felt. "Never mind. You don't have to twist my arm. I've been salivating for the last ten minutes." He'd been drooling over her, but he wasn't going to tell her that. If he did . . . No, he wouldn't do it. He'd eat dinner, draw her out about Dunn, and go back to the motel. *Forget about sex*, he ordered himself. Forget about Gracie. Concentrate on the food or the case or anything but his own aching body parts.

They sat down to dinner, neither speaking for the next few minutes. Max was too busy savoring the best chicken casserole he'd eaten since his grandma's cooking. After taking the edge off his hunger, he broke the silence. "Does Dunn sic his dogs on everybody he doesn't like or am I just lucky?"

Gracie glanced up from her plate. "You're just lucky." A corner of her mouth lifted. "Besides, we don't know that Leroy is behind this. You can't even tell me for certain what kind of dogs they were."

"Are you so sure he's not involved?"

She took a bite of casserole and looked thoughtful. "Leroy's a good deputy. He does his job."

"You sound like you're trying to convince yourself of that. And you didn't answer the question."

Her expression grew more troubled. "I don't always agree with everything he does, but then, he doesn't always agree with me either. And Leroy's—" She hesitated and finished, "loyal."

Max found that an interesting statement, especially since she'd yet to answer his question directly. "Loyal? To you?"

Setting her fork down, she met his eyes. "I told you about my father. Leroy was his deputy when he was charged with taking bribes. He stood behind Dad the whole time, never once admitted there was a possibility of my father's guilt. That meant a lot to my father, and to me. Even though Leroy has his faults, I can't forget that."

"Minor little faults like setting his dogs on a person," Max couldn't resist saying.

"I do my job, Max." She met his ironic look with an unsmiling face. "Don't worry, I'll be checking it out. Remember, just because you don't like him doesn't mean he did it."

Max shrugged. "What's to like? He threw me in jail."

She laughed, chasing away the shadows in her eyes. "So did I."

Laughter transformed her face, and he couldn't help staring at her, fascinated. "Yeah, but you're a lot prettier than he is." Her ready blush made him grin. There he went again, flirting with her when he should be sticking to business. But she looked so damn cute when he said things that flustered her, he couldn't resist.

Flirting was a big mistake, though. It led to thoughts of getting her into bed with him, which wasn't at all what he ought to be thinking about.

Except that he was.

Somehow he made it through the rest of dinner. Through the sight of the creamy skin of her chest, the rise and fall of her delectable breasts when she laughed. Through the feel of those same breasts brushing his arm when she gave him another helping of mouthwatering casserole. Through the sight of those dark brown eyes sparkling with life, and her wide, beautiful mouth, tempting him to say to hell with his scruples and make love to her anyway.

Max carried his dishes to the sink and stood staring down at them. He figured he had about two minutes before he lost whatever shreds of willpower he had left. "Thanks for dinner. Would you mind taking me back to the motel?"

"If that's what you want."

He turned his head to find her a few inches away from him, smiling. What he *wanted* was to tuck the swing of mahogany hair behind her ear, pull her close and kiss her until both of them stopped thinking. What he *wanted* was to feel her skin against his, heat against heat. What he wanted wasn't going to happen.

Her smile was pure female. Mysterious, seductive. He found it hard to breathe, and it wasn't because he'd eaten too much. "Damn, Gracie, don't do that," he grated out.

"Don't do what?" she asked, her voice like cool satin, tempting as the night.

He gripped the edge of the counter. "I'm having a hell of a time keeping my hands off you. If you keep looking at me like that . . ."

"Like what?"

Like she wanted to throw him down and have her way with him, he thought. Mesmerized, he swallowed hard and stared at her.

Another step brought her even nearer. "What if I want your hands on me?" She laid her palms on his chest and spread her fingers across it. "What if I want to put my hands on you?"

Her face was tilted up to his. Her mouth was close, so close, he could feel her warm breath feather across his lips. He could smell her, that fresh, clean smell that was only hers. And he could see desire darkening her eyes to burnt umber.

Only a saint could have resisted Gracie just then, and Max was no saint. He crushed her mouth beneath his, parting her lips, sliding his tongue in and out in a slow, primal rhythm. She tasted like desire itself. Need, more than he wanted to feel, shot through him, slamming a hard fist into his belly.

The low, throaty moan she gave almost did him in. Her fingers stabbed through his hair, her breasts pressed against his chest, her mouth moved under his, wild and greedy. He pulled her against him, cupping her bottom through the short skirt, then reaching beneath it to stroke her hips, bare except for a thin, silky strip of panties.

Slow down, he thought, and moved his hands to her chest. To breasts that had taunted him all night until he thought he'd go insane if he didn't touch them. He stopped kissing her so he could watch her face as he plunged his hands inside the low-cut neckline of her blouse, inside the lacy bra, and filled them with her warm, beautiful breasts.

Her eyes widened with shock, then glazed with desire as he cupped her breasts and rubbed the hardening nipples with his palms. Her breath came now in panting gasps. He wanted her naked, stretched out beneath him. Wanted to see the dazed pleasure in her eyes as he brought her to climax. Wanted to lose himself in her. In her passion, and his.

But she had to be as sure as he was.

Groaning, he pulled his hands from beneath her blouse and buried his face between her neck and shoulder. His hands dropped to her waist. "Gracie, wait."

Wait? Not again, she thought. *Please tell me he's not going to stop again.* Gracie had never imagined that a man could make her giddy and breathless, hot and trembling all at once, but Max made her feel all that, and more. Her breasts ached, longing for him to touch them again. Her entire body ached for his touch. He still held her at the waist, though he'd pushed her away from him.

"You need to be sure about this."

She started to answer, but he hushed her, laying his fingers on her lips.

"Making love won't change anything. I'll still be leaving when my job is finished. A few days, a few weeks, but then I'll be gone."

She couldn't stop a pang of longing, even as she appreciated his candor. Was she being a fool, giving herself to a man who had admitted that all he wanted from their relationship was sex? A man who had no interest in anything lasting? Did she?

It shocked her to realize that sensible Grace O'Malley was contemplating having a wild fling with a man. With Max. Could it be so much worse than wondering if she would ever be like other women, feel like other women? If she didn't seize the moment, would she ever feel like this again? Want like this again?

She drew in a deep breath and smiled. "I'm sure," she said. "Are you?"

That lady-killer smile flashed just before his mouth took hers. He kissed her as no one ever had before. Hot, hard, hungry. Like he wanted her, and meant to have her.

Her senses swam, her blood hummed, heating to a fever pitch. His hands streaked underneath her blouse, flicked open her bra, and covered her bare breasts once again. Strong, work-roughened hands caressed her, his fingers pulling gently at her nipples. She heard a strangled moan and realized it was hers.

His hands fell to massage her rear, pulling her closer to him. He slid them beneath her skirt, murmuring hot words as he cupped and caressed her bottom through her satin panties, before he slipped one hand between her legs to stroke. She felt him harden against her stomach and sucked in air, trying to catch her breath.

His voice deep, seductive, he spoke in her ear. "Take me to your bedroom."

She'd have gone anywhere he asked just then. She managed to nod and lead him out of the kitchen toward the bedroom. By the time they reached it, her blouse and bra were gone, abandoned along the way.

Max reached across her to flip on the bedside light. "That's better. Now I can see you."

Gracie fought the urge to cover herself as his gaze journeyed over her lingeringly, but the hot passion in his eyes reassured her that he wasn't thinking of her imperfections. Her fingers wouldn't cooperate when she attacked the buttons of his shirt. He helped her, flinging the shirt away before he tumbled her onto the bed, his thighs settling between hers as though he belonged there.

His mouth clamped hard over her bare nipple. Her back arched, and she nearly screamed at the blinding flash of elation that tore through her. She clasped his head to her breast, sinking her fingers into his black, silky hair. His tongue flicked over her nipple, once, twice, bringing it to a peak before he moved to the other one. Each rasp of his tongue, the touch of his lips to her skin brought new sensations, exciting, dizzying waves of intensity.

She protested faintly when he moved from between her legs, choking it off when she felt his hand sliding inside her panties. Involuntarily, her hips lifted, then his finger slid deep inside her, making the ache both better and more intense.

"That's it, darlin'," he said. "You like that, don't you?"

Like it? Oh, Lord, she'd never imagined feelings like the ones bombarding her. All she could manage was a long moan as her eyes closed. His finger withdrew and thrust in again and again, until she thought she'd die from pleasure.

He unbuttoned and unzipped her skirt, peeling it down her hips and legs, taking her panties along with it until she lay naked on the bed. His weight shifted. She opened her eyes to see him standing beside the bed, watching her as he stripped his jeans and briefs off.

Lord, he was beautiful, she thought, unable to stop staring at him. Her gaze swept from his broad chest to the ridges of his abdomen, down to narrow hips, powerful thighs, and an erection that flat took her breath away. Her eyes widened, she'd had no idea a fully aroused male would be quite so . . . impressive. There was no possible way he was going to fit inside of her.

His lips curved upward, a devilish gleam entering his eyes. "You don't look so sure anymore."

"I—you—I don't think you'll fit," she blurted out, flushing.

Those gorgeous blue eyes flashed, his dimple winked. "Don't worry, darlin', I'll fit. We'll make sure of it." Reaching down, he picked up his jeans and pulled out his wallet, taking a foil packet from it and tossing it down on the bedside table.

"I've never been very good at resisting temptation," he said at her questioning look. "And you're one hell of a temptation, Gracie."

A temptation. Max thought she was a temptation. Oh, she liked the sound of that. Smiling, she held out her hand to him.

He came down beside her on the bed, gathering her into his arms as his mouth covered hers in a hungry kiss. His hand parted her legs, and once again his fingers probed her heated flesh. Lifting her hips to meet the motions of his hand, she caressed his chest, savoring the feel of his smooth, warm skin, the sleek muscles that rippled beneath her touch.

"You're tight as a virgin," he murmured, kissing her breast while his fingers continued their erotic movements.

Dimly she heard the words and knew she should tell him, but he'd pushed her so high, she thought she'd shatter. She couldn't form the words. He groaned and rolled away from her, grabbing the condom from the table and ripping the package open.

"Max, there's—I'm—" Floundering for words, she watched as he fit the protection over himself. "I've—"

He cut her off with a passionate kiss, drew back and lifted her hips, then filled her with a solid, driving thrust. She cried out at the flash of pain, even as it was already fading. Max froze, staring down at her, his eyes shocked, stunned.

Dazed, she stared back at him. Never in her life had she felt like this. This sense of wonder, sense of completion. Everything bright, new, exciting. When he entered her she'd felt pain, but now . . . It was supposed to hurt, wasn't it? But oh, she didn't hurt at all. She'd found something she hadn't even known she was missing.

Raising her hips, tightening her muscles, she saw Max struggle for control. She didn't want him controlled. She wanted him to feel as wild as she did. Wanted him to feel the same reckless abandon she felt. She, Grace O'Malley, who'd never been reckless or abandoned in her life.

"Gracie." His voice sounded harsh and strained. "God, don't do that. If you don't stop— Stop . . . moving like—"

Ignoring him, she pressed her hips against his. He groaned, surrendering to the inevitable. She wrapped her arms and legs around him, holding tight as he stroked in and out of her. Slow, deep thrusts that grew faster, deeper, his eyes never straying from her face as he sent her climbing higher and higher. Shocking her with its force and its sudden, almost painful peaking, her climax hit hard and fast, rolling through her like a tidal wave before she cried out and came apart.

Max pushed in, withdrew, sank into her again with a final plunge, his body going rigid, his head buried between her neck and shoulder. She felt him shudder, spend himself inside her, then finally, he stilled.

EIGHT

Forcing himself to move, Max rolled over to lie beside Gracie on the bed. As he stared at the ceiling, the same questions played over and over in his mind. What had he done? What had he been thinking?

Hell, thinking hadn't entered into it. He'd wanted her too damned badly to think at all. If he had stopped to consider, even for a moment, he would have recognized the signs. No wonder she'd seemed so shy at times. Innocent. Untouched. Gracie *was* innocent. Or she had been, until he'd come along and—

"What's wrong?" she asked, interrupting his litany of self-castigation. "Didn't you like it?"

Shocked at the question, he turned his head to stare at her. "Like it? Did I like making love to you?"

Having risen on her elbow to look at him, she

nodded. Her face still held a glow—the glow of passion slaked. She looked tumbled, drowsy, and so damn sexy he wanted her again. Now.

He scowled. "Of course I liked it. It was fantastic. Amazing. But that's not the point."

Her lips curved into a smug smile. "Fantastic. Hmm, I like that. I thought so too." The smile took on a seductive tilt.

His stomach clenched. "Stop smiling at me like that." No way, he wouldn't do it again.

"Why? That's what I do when I'm happy."

"You should be upset. Angry. Anything but happy." He got out of bed and grabbed his jeans. "I'm not the man you should have chosen to be your first." An understatement if he'd ever heard one. Stepping into his pants, he jerked them up over his hips and zipped them.

"You're exactly the man I should have chosen. You made it wonderful for me."

"You're not experienced enough to make that call." He strode to the bathroom, returning a minute later with a warm, wet washcloth. "Here," he said, handing it to her.

Unwilling to watch her wash away the evidence of her innocence, he paced the room, raking his hands through his hair. "Good God, a virgin," he muttered.

"We might be a dying breed, but there are still some of us around," she said dryly.

Over his shoulder, he shot her a grim look. "Yeah, well, there's one less now."

"It's not a disease, Max. Haven't you ever been with a virgin before?"

His back to her once again, he nearly laughed. Since Marla's death his lovers had invariably been experienced women who knew what they wanted and agreed with his terms. No emotional involvement, just good sex. Gracie didn't know those rules.

"Not in years," he said. "Not since my wife."

"You're . . . married?"

At the whispered distress in her voice, he turned around to look at her. The washcloth, tinged with her blood, lay on the floor beside the bed. She'd pulled the sheet up over her breasts and was clutching it to her chest. Her expression held shock, dismay—and to his shame, self-blame. Great, now she thought he was a philanderer. And blamed herself for sleeping with him, no doubt. Even if he *was* a defiler of innocents, he could set her mind at rest about one thing.

He walked back to the bed and looked down at her. "Was married. She died." He didn't add that the marriage had died long before his wife had.

Gracie's hand settled on his arm, offering comfort. "I'm sorry. Was it—?" She hesitated, searching for words. "Did you lose her recently?"

Her gaze fixed on his, her eyes filled with empathy, compassion. Gracie's compassion. The very last thing in the world he deserved. "No. It was a long time ago."

"You must have loved her very much." Her

voice was soft and husky with sympathy. Offering comfort, one of those gifts of emotion she shared so generously.

"I didn't love her at all," he said bluntly, and pulled away from her. He said it as much to shock her out of her rosy-hued view of him as anything else. But she didn't look shocked, she simply looked . . . thoughtful.

Dammit, why couldn't he just let it go at that? Sighing, he sat beside her on the bed and found himself telling her more, though he'd had no intention of ever discussing his marriage or Marla's death with anyone.

"She—Marla—had problems with my career. Major problems. We'd been fighting for months and were on the verge of divorce when she got sick. Then we found out she had cancer. Ovarian cancer. We decided to stay together. She—she died a year after that." Even now, ten long years later, he blocked that time of his life from his memory. It was a miserable, dark time he had no intention of reliving.

"If you didn't love her, why did you stay with her?"

Gracie's eyes were two huge pools of understanding. He fell into the well without meaning to, without wanting to. "The doctors discovered she was terminal pretty quickly. Staying seemed like the right thing to do." And Max had always done the right thing. Back then, anyway. No longer.

Seducing Gracie sure as hell hadn't been *the right thing* to do.

"But we were talking about you, not me," he said abruptly, angry with her and himself for bringing up something he'd thought long buried.

"Have you lost all your senses?" he demanded. "Gracie, I told you I'm leaving when my job is finished. This"—he gestured at the rumpled bed—"doesn't change anything. I meant what I said, I'm still leaving." After he finished his investigation of the woman he'd just deflowered. *Prime move, Max.*

She lifted her chin and met his gaze. "Yes, you told me. Give me some credit, Max. I may have been a virgin, but I'm not a fool. I knew exactly what I was doing."

She obviously thought so, but he knew better. He cupped her cheek in the palm of his hand, rubbing his thumb over her mouth. "Why didn't you tell me? You should have told me. I wasn't gentle. I must have hurt you."

"You didn't hurt me. I thought it was supposed to, but—" She gave him another of those blinding smiles. "I liked it. And I didn't think you'd make love to me if I told you."

He dropped his hand. "You're damned right I wouldn't have." Because he didn't want the responsibility of taking a woman's virginity. Taking a woman's innocence made him feel trapped. If you took a woman's virginity, you should be willing to do the right thing by her. And he couldn't, not this time. Too late, though. Much too late. He'd already done it.

"There you go. See, I made the right choice." Brushing her hair away from her face, she tilted her head back to gaze at him triumphantly.

Curbing a swift stab of lust at the sight of her bare neck and shoulders above the white sheet, Max frowned. "You made a ridiculous choice. If I'd ever imagined . . . I knew you were inexperienced but—Good God, Gracie, how have you reached your age without ever making love? You must be, what, twenty-seven, twenty-eight?"

Those gorgeous lips curved into an enticing smile. Too enticing. His gaze dropped, and he swallowed hard. The sheet had slipped down to expose her breasts and the smooth skin of her belly. Bare, dusky nipples invited him to touch, caress, taste. His mouth went dry. *Forget it, Max,* he told himself, closing his eyes. *You will not make love to her again. You absolutely will not—*

"I'm thirty-one," she said.

His eyes snapped open, and he stared at her.

"Thanks," she added, with an impudent grin.

Searching her face, he asked the question that had nagged him since he'd recovered enough to wonder how the hell she could have been a virgin. "Why me?"

Please God, he thought, don't let her tell him she loved him. He'd already done an unconscionable thing, seducing a woman under his investigation, even though he knew she was as innocent of smuggling aliens as she'd been of a man's touch. Until his.

"I wanted you."

Her words, spoken in that husky drawl, shot a shaft of desire straight to his loins. Did she have any idea how sexy she looked, lying in that rumpled bed with only half a sheet for cover? Her lips swollen, her breasts flushed, her short dark hair tousled from his hands. No, Gracie wasn't beautiful, but God, she was sexy. His blood heated, throbbed in his veins. His heart rate increased, and he felt himself getting hard. Dammit, he'd made love to her once. It should have been enough.

It wasn't.

"I never understood what all the fuss was about," she said in a musing tone. "Never cared that much to find out, either. Until you." The look she sent him held pure, feminine satisfaction.

"Don't look at me like that, Gracie," he warned her. "I told you before, I've never been good at resisting temptation."

"Nobody's asking you to resist. Seems to me I'm asking just the opposite."

Inspired, desperately grasping, he said, "We can't. I only had one condom."

"Look in the drawer." She pointed at the bedside table.

He looked inside and groaned. A full box. Lord have mercy, he thought, struggling with the ideas that box brought to mind. "We shouldn't," he said, knowing he was fighting a losing battle.

"Why not?" Her voice held laughter, and so did her eyes.

There were reasons. He knew there were reasons, even if he couldn't think of them now. "Dammit, Gracie, you know—"

"Max. Anybody ever tell you, you talk too much?" She drew the sheet away from herself, her body stretched out along the mattress, gleaming pale ivory in the glow of the lamplight. "Make love with me again."

Her voice seemed to surround him, as tempting as a summer dream. A man could resist only so much. He'd no doubt roast in hell for what he was about to do, but he was headed that way already. Might as well make certain of it. Smiling, he stretched out beside her and took her in his arms. "You're a dangerous woman, Grace O'Malley."

"No more talking," she whispered, and pressed her lips to his.

Late the next afternoon Gracie stopped at the diner for her customary cup of coffee. "Con, you around?" she called out.

"Be there in a second," came Connie's voice from the kitchen.

Gracie helped herself, carrying the cup with her to her favorite booth, one of the few with a level table. As usual, the brew was strong enough to walk on its own, but Gracie liked it that way. She still missed having a cigarette to go with it. Since meeting Max though, her former habit hadn't been on her mind nearly as often. She'd even managed to quit chewing so much gum.

Ceiling fans whirred lazily, stirring the air even if they didn't do much to cool it. Too late for lunch, too early for dinner, so she and Connie were alone in the diner. Gracie liked this time of day, finding it a quiet, thoughtful time. Today, though, she couldn't keep her mind on anything except the night before. She smiled as one particular memory came to mind.

"Obviously, it worked."

Gracie started in surprise as Connie sat down across from her. Her smile widened before the sight of her friend's face reminded her of what else had been going on lately. "Thanks, Connie."

"I'm not so sure I did you a favor," Connie said. "Good Lord, Gracie, I've never seen you look this way before."

"What way?"

"You're in love with him. Oh, I should never have helped you. I should have known you'd fall in love."

Gracie opened her mouth to deny the charge, then shut it with a snap. Connie was one-hundred-percent right. She had fallen in love with him.

Max made her feel . . . like a woman. Treated her like a woman. Not like the sheriff, or a friend, but as a desirable woman. He was the only man who'd ever looked beneath the badge to her heart.

"You're not even going to deny it, are you?"

"Nope." She shook her head and grinned. "You're right. I am in love with him."

"Honey." Connie's voice gentled, her eyes filled with compassion. "He told you he wasn't sticking around. This isn't a good thing."

"Con, I know you worry about me, but I'm fine. It was wonderful. Even if he leaves tomorrow, it was worth it."

"You won't think that when he leaves you with a broken heart," she said flatly.

"Maybe. But maybe he won't end up leaving."

"That bum didn't tell you he loved you, did he?" Indignantly, Connie got to her feet. "Let me at him!"

Gracie laughed. "He didn't take advantage of me. And no, he doesn't love me. Not yet."

Connie waggled a warning finger at her. "Girlfriend, you're riding for a fall. I know men like him. He'll be fun and charming, show you a great time. It'll be incredible. And then he'll walk out. At least he'll have warned you before he does it."

"People change. Maybe Max will."

Sinking back into the seat, Connie passed her hand over her eyes. "Lord, listen to her. She's dreaming."

"No harm in dreams," Gracie said. "It's when your dreams die that trouble comes along."

"Were you at least careful? Tell me you were careful."

Exasperated, Gracie sighed. "Yes, Mama." At the time, she had thought Connie was crazy to insist on giving her a full box of condoms, along with a lecture to use them, but she'd been right. Thinking about it, Gracie smiled.

"Earth to Gracie," Connie drawled. "How about checking in with reality for a while?"

"I don't think I'm being all that unrealistic." Or was she? "Max has been married before. It's not like he's never made a commitment." He hadn't loved his wife, he'd said, but he'd stayed with her because she was dying. In Gracie's book that meant commitment.

"He's divorced?"

She shook her head. "His wife died, a long time ago, he said. It bothers him still, I think, more than he lets on. He didn't talk much about it."

"Wonderful," Connie snapped. "A man who's hung up on his dead wife. That's just peachy. I don't know where my mind was that night we talked."

"Maybe on your own problems." Connie didn't answer, but a flush rose in her cheeks. The swelling had gone down and her bruises had faded, but they were still plainly seen. "Want to tell me about it?" Gracie asked quietly.

The chimes jingled just then, drawing both their gazes toward the doorway where Leroy Dunn stood. Connie's eyes widened, training on him like a trapped rabbit's.

Leroy didn't say a word, just jerked his head toward the swinging doors to the kitchen and walked through them. Connie rose like she was a frog and he'd told her to leap.

"I need to talk to him," she said to Gracie.

Gracie grasped her friend's hand, restraining her. "He doesn't have any hold over you, no matter what's happened. You know that, don't you?"

Connie's eyes were as bleak as her voice. "It's not what you think, Gracie."

But it was, Gracie thought, watching her friend walk away.

Gracie believed in honest confrontation, but sometimes a person wasn't offered that choice. Still, she hadn't intended to eavesdrop. It wasn't her fault that she needed more coffee. Or that the hot plate with the pot was over by the kitchen doors—the same doors Connie and Leroy had disappeared behind a minute earlier. And it sure as heck wasn't her fault that she heard some of what they said, since when she was mad Connie's voice was louder than a hog caller's in the finals at the county fair.

"What we talked about is none of your business," Connie was saying. "Who do you think you are, telling me what I can and can't say? She's my best friend, and I'll see her whenever I damn well please. And say whatever I damn well want to. You don't own me, Leroy Dunn, so you can just—"

Gracie couldn't hear Leroy's reply, only the deep rumble of his voice. Wishing he'd speak up, she edged toward the crack between the doors and tilted her head to angle her ear closer. Strain as she might, for the next couple of minutes she couldn't make out anything they were saying.

Then Connie shouted, "If you think you can tell me what to do, think again! I'm not somebody you can toss in a cell and tell to shut up."

"Chapman" was the only word that came through clearly in Leroy's reply.

"You wouldn't dare," Connie said. "Not with what I know."

"You don't know squat. Don't cross me, Connie May, or you'll be sorry," Leroy said, his voice louder than it had been yet. "Sorrier than you were the other night."

Good Lord, Gracie realized, he was right by the door. She scrambled out of the way just as the swinging doors crashed back against the wall.

At the sight of her standing a couple of feet away, Leroy stopped. "Hear everything you wanted to, Sheriff?" he asked with an ugly sneer as he looked her up and down.

Gracie raised her chin and met his eyes. "As a matter of fact, no."

NINE

Dunn nearly mowed Max down as he blasted out of the diner. Wondering what had set the deputy off, Max stepped inside and found out.

Tension simmered in the air, obvious amidst the placid whir of the ceiling fans in the dead quiet room. With her back to him, Gracie blocked the kitchen doorway. Her friend Connie faced her with her chin angled up truculently. The bruises on the redhead's face and Dunn's hasty exit went a long way toward explaining the strained atmosphere. Neither woman seemed to know, or care, that he was there.

"I want to talk to you," Gracie said grimly.

"I can't talk about it. The best thing you can do is forget whatever you heard."

"Like heck I will." Slapping her hands on her hips, Gracie widened her stance. "Yes, I heard some of that little scene between you and Leroy.

Now, you tell me what's going on, Connie May, and you tell me right now. I mean it."

"Ask Leroy."

Gracie waited a beat and said, "All right, I will."

Alarm changed Connie's expression so fast, it was almost comical. Would have been if the subject hadn't been such an obviously loaded one.

"I didn't—I didn't mean that," she stammered. "You'll only make things worse. Just leave it alone, Gracie. Please." Casting her an agonized glance, Connie shoved past her and fled toward the back.

Jaw clenched, Gracie turned and glared after her friend. Max could almost hear her teeth grind. He'd seen her angry before, about the dog, but it had been a different anger than what he saw now. Wanting to ease her frustration, he touched her arm, squeezing it when she whirled to face him.

"Easy. It's just me."

"How long have you been standing there?"

He lifted a shoulder. "Long enough. Need to talk?"

"I probably shouldn't," she said, taking a furious spin around the room before returning to where he stood. "But if I don't talk to someone I might start screaming."

Max guided her to a counter stool and took the one beside it. "So, tell me about it. Lover's quarrel?"

"That's sure what it looked like," Gracie said

bitterly. "Problem is, Leroy's the wrong lover. Connie's engaged to Reese Chapman."

"The old man?" Max asked incredulously. "No wonder she's messing—"

"Not him. Connie's engaged to his son."

"Is that who did the number on her face?"

She shook her head. "Leroy did that the other night. That's one thing I'm sure of now. But she won't tell me or talk about it. Claims she ran into a door."

Max raised an eyebrow. "Right. Do you have any idea what they were fighting about just now?"

"Not really. I, uh—I couldn't hear much of what they were saying."

"Poor eavesdropping skills?" he asked, his lips twitching.

A little shamefaced, she said, "I'm not proud of it, but I couldn't think of any other way to get information. From what I can figure, Connie knows something about Leroy that he doesn't want made public. And it's plain as peaches what Leroy was threatening her with."

"Maybe she doesn't care if her fiancé finds out she's cheating—"

"She cares," Gracie interrupted, getting up to pace again. "Believe me, she cares. I don't know why she's taken up with Leroy when I know she loves Reese."

Watching her, Max shrugged. "Who knows? Fun, excitement. Thrill of the forbidden. Although," he added dryly, "Deputy Dog doesn't look like much fun to me."

Her fists clenched. "Me either. Connie's being a fool. If Reese finds out, I hope he can forgive her."

"Men have forgiven worse," Max said cynically. "And so have women."

"Would you?"

Their eyes met. He wasn't sure how to answer that, so he gave her the truth. "Since I don't plan on having a fiancée again, I'm not sure it matters."

"You were married. What about your wife? Would you have forgiven her?"

"I don't know." His expression grew grim, his gaze still locked with hers. "That wasn't one of our problems."

Gracie closed her eyes and bowed her head, passing a hand over her brow. "I'm sorry. I had no business asking you that. I'm so dadblamed mad and frustrated, I don't know what to do. It makes me crazy when my friends do stupid things."

He stood and walked over to her. "You aren't responsible for Connie's choices."

"I know that. But she's as close as I've got to family and I'm not going to sit by while she ruins her life. Not without at least trying to stop her."

Taking her face in his hands, he tilted it back and gazed down into her eyes. He wanted to comfort her, wanted to erase the lines of stress and worry that furrowed her brow. He lowered his head and touched his lips to hers, felt them part as she sighed into his mouth.

Door chimes jingled, reminding him of where they were. Reluctantly, he raised his head and let his hands drop. Gracie blushed adorably, and he grinned.

"Oh, my stars," Maude babbled. "Dear me, I didn't mean to—I just stopped by for a cup of coffee and some of that delicious peach pie. Don't mind me."

"Let me get it for you, Maude," Gracie said, moving fast in her confusion. "Connie's in the back."

Max eyed Maude warily while Gracie went to the kitchen. The postmistress reminded him of a fluttery bird as she twittered, twitched, and flitted around, stumbling into him on her way to the counter. A sparrow, maybe. At the moment, an apprehensive sparrow. Checking his back pocket, he felt the outline of his wallet. He couldn't help smiling and was rewarded by a huge sigh of relief and an answering smile.

"Here you go." Grace set Maude's order on the counter in front of her.

"I've got to get back to work," she added to Max, walking with him to the door. "Did you want some pie too? Is that why you came over?"

"Actually, I was looking for you. Your jailer said you'd be here. I wanted to take you to dinner tonight. There's a Mexican place about twenty miles from here that's supposed to be dynamite."

Her eyes lit with pleasure before disappointment shadowed them. "I can't, I'm working."

"Maybe tomorrow, then," he said, surprised at his own level of disappointment. What was one night? Especially when he ought to be backing off anyway, instead of becoming more involved.

As he left, Max patted his back pocket again, satisfied that at least this time Maude hadn't hijacked his wallet.

Through a haze of deep brown eyes, fragrant skin, long legs tangled with his, Max struggled to wake. Confused, he sat up and rubbed his eyes. A dream, he thought. Oh, man, what a dream. About Gracie. Making love with Gracie.

Thanks to Maude's itchy fingers, he had no watch to tell him the time, but the clock on the bedside table read 11:14 P.M. Focused on the wallet, he hadn't thought to check his wrist until much later. Someone knocked at his door, and he realized that must be what had awakened him.

"Hang on," he said, killing the TV before he dragged on his jeans, zipping them as he crossed the room. He swung the door wide to see Gracie standing underneath the yellow light cast by a naked bulb. She wore her uniform, minus the hat and gun belt, and in his current highly charged state, she looked good enough to devour.

"I got you out of bed, didn't I?" She smiled ruefully. "I'm sorry. Your light was on, so I thought you were still awake. Do you want me to let you go back to sleep?"

That whiskey-flavored drawl of hers did something to his gut. Coupled with the dream he'd just had, it did something to other parts of his anatomy as well. Shaking his head to clear it, he stepped back and let her in. "I fell asleep watching the tube. Didn't you have to work?"

"Leroy took the late shift," she said. "Seemed like the least he could do." Apparently undecided whether to stand or sit, she looked around.

He couldn't blame her. Seeing the room through Gracie's eyes, he wished he'd bothered to pick up some of the dirty clothes and newspaper thrown around. "Sorry. I'm not usually this much of a slob. If I'd known you were coming . . ." Allowing the sentence to trail off, he bent to grab a gray T-shirt and toss it in the corner on top of what passed for a laundry pile.

"Hey, don't clean up for me." She laid a hand on his arm to stop him.

Disoriented from sleep, the dream, her soap-and-water scent, he froze at the contact. All she'd done was touch his arm. Get a grip, he told himself. Of course, if he hadn't woken up dreaming about her and hard as a rock, it would have been a lot easier to do that.

"I shouldn't have come so late, but I wanted to see you." She smiled, and he sank like a stone to the bottom of the lake. A smile of pure happiness. At seeing him.

It blew him away. He couldn't remember the last time anyone had taken that much pleasure in his company. *Leave her alone*, he told himself. *Back off now, before you get in even deeper.* His gaze locked with hers, and all he could think was how good it had felt to hold her the night before, how good it would feel to do so again.

Then she put her arms around his neck and kissed him, and he knew he'd lost the battle, if not the entire war. Groaning, he gave in and wrapped her in his arms, crushing her to his bare chest. Their tongues met, twined together while he cupped her bottom and pressed her against the raging ache. Her head fell back as he tasted her throat, taking little nips with his teeth, then soothing them with his tongue.

She laughed shakily. "You had me worried for a"—her breath hitched as his hand closed over her breast and squeezed—"minute. I thought you were going to boot me out of here."

"Not a chance." He jerked her shirt out of her slacks and unbuttoned it quickly, filling his hands with her breasts for a moment before he flicked open her bra and slid everything off. Beautiful breasts, he thought, watching the flush of desire cover her chest, and bent his head to capture one upthrust crest.

"I've thought about this all day," she said on a throaty sigh of pleasure. His tongue rasped her nipple. It budded tightly as he drew it into his mouth, sucking strongly. Using one hand to plump up her other breast, he rolled her nipple with his fingers until she arched her back to offer him more.

He trailed his lips up her chest to her throat, resting at the hollow where her pulse beat fast and thready. "I kept telling myself," she said, her hands attacking his zipper with frantic determination, "that it couldn't have been this good." She pulled his zipper down, slipped her hand inside his jeans, and closed it around him. "But it was."

Good didn't even touch it. He almost lost it right there, especially when she slowly stroked her hand up and down his length and the peaks of her breasts burned against his naked chest. They both groaned. To have been a virgin the day before, she sure learned fast. "Gracie, slow down."

"Do I have to?" She buried her face in his neck and kissed him, small nips and bites like those he'd tortured her with a minute ago.

God, she was going to kill him. Removing her hands from inside his jeans, he placed them on his chest instead. Then he reached for her slacks, unzipped them, dragged them and her plain white cotton panties down her hips. Slid his hand between her thighs and probed her slick flesh. Hot. Tight.

She was ready for him, he could feel it in the way her hips bucked against his hand, hear it in the choked-off moans coming from her throat. He boosted her up onto the low dresser and picked up her foot, jerking first one boot off, then the other, before he finished yanking off the rest of her clothes.

He didn't remove his jeans, needing that last barrier to maintain the control he was barely hanging on to. Her legs wrapped tight around him, skin against skin. He took her mouth, tasted the sweet, brimming heat of desire, drowned in the thrust and parry of her tongue mating with his.

"Now, Max. Don't make me wait," she whispered.

Forget control, he thought. In a heartbeat, he shucked his jeans and briefs. They stared into each other's eyes as he halted just short of sinking himself to the hilt inside her. *Oh, God, no.* He'd almost forgotten protection. Stopping just then seemed . . . impossible. She was so tempting, so ready, a seductive feast waiting for him to savor her. If he didn't take her right now, he'd die.

The trust in her eyes snapped him back to sanity. "Dammit!" Cursing again, he shoved himself away. "Don't move," he ordered, and made it to the bathroom in two strides. He dumped the contents of his shaving kit in the sink, scrambling until he found the condoms.

She was just as he'd left her, naked and waiting for him, her brown eyes wide and dazed with passion. Seconds later she opened to him and he buried himself inside her. A warm, wet, welcoming fantasy, she tightened around him. Only she was reality, not illusion. He pulled out, then slowly filled her again, watching her eyes glaze as he did so. "Again," he murmured, and sank inside her while her nails dug into his shoulders and her breath came in gasps.

He couldn't keep the pace slow for long, not with the sexy whimpers coming from her throat driving him over the top. Not with the way her back arched and her hips met his until he didn't think he'd last another minute. He crushed her hard against him, taking her mouth as she came, drinking in her cry of completion and with a final heave, exploded inside her moments later.

When he could move, he carried her to the bed. She lay beside him, gazing at him, her eyes huge dark pools of sated passion. And he was very much afraid another emotion played in those beautiful eyes alongside the desire.

"I love you, Max," she said.

Exactly what he'd been afraid of. Why, then, did hearing the words make him feel so good? Why did it make him . . . happy? This was a disaster, for Gracie, at least. "Gracie—"

She laid her fingers on his lips. "You're not going to tell me that what I'm really feeling is just lust, are you?"

He wanted to, but he didn't believe it any more than she did. He kissed her fingers, then held them. "I wish I could, but it wouldn't do any good, would it?"

Smiling at him, she shook her head.

"The problem is, I'm not ready—hell, I'll

never be ready—to get involved with anyone. I've done that once, I can't do it again. I'm leaving, Gracie, and I'm not coming back."

"I know. You told me. It's all right, Max. I knew the rules going in." She sat up against the headboard, pulling the sheet over herself.

He sat up as well. "The hell you did. You were a virgin." And he was a rotten slime to have taken advantage of her. "I was the experienced one, and I should have known better. I did know better, but I wanted you, so I—"

"You were honest with me," she interrupted. "It's not your fault, or your problem."

His stomach rolled with nausea. Right, he'd been real honest with her, lying to her from day one. Lying to her still. "Dammit, I should never have touched you in the first place."

"Well . . ." She slid him a mischievous look. "I do believe I did a lot of encouraging."

"I should leave you the hell alone."

"Are you going to?"

Staring into her eyes, he slowly shook his head.

"Good."

He pulled her into his arms and kissed her, holding her close. He wanted her. She was warm, giving, yielding, and he wanted to bury himself inside the sweet welcome of her body; wanted, for the few days or weeks that they had together, to accept the love she offered. And she wanted him.

He could feel it in the give of her body, in the pull of her lips, in the touch of her tongue against his. Oh, yeah, she wanted him—but would she be so loving if she knew the truth? If she knew he was a liar—and worse?

TEN

Max woke the next morning groggy from lack of sleep. Making love with Gracie most of the night before was to blame for that, but he'd spent the early-morning hours after she left tossing and turning, guilt eating him alive. No matter how he tried, he couldn't justify what he was doing to Gracie. But he couldn't seem to leave her alone, either.

A shower chased away his listlessness, but it didn't improve his mood. As he began to shave, he stared into the mirror. Gracie's face gazed back at him. Her mouth, soft and swollen from his kisses; her eyes, filling with dazed pleasure as he slid inside her. He winced as he nicked himself. Damn, this wasn't helping.

She'd said she loved him. And he suspected that he was a lot more attached to her than was good for him. He knew he wasn't ready for anything lasting, and never would be. He'd done that once and it had ended in disaster—and death. No way in hell was he willing to try it again. Not even for Gracie, as sweet, loving, and decent a woman as he'd ever known.

While dressing, his uneasiness hardened into resolve. He would find some kind of evidence to back up his theories about the smuggling ring, then he would get the hell out of Hell, just as he'd intended from the outset. The sooner he left, the sooner Gracie would get over him.

First he stopped by the post office to retrieve his watch. The engraved watch his parents had given him when he became a Ranger. Stupidly, it hadn't occurred to him to leave it at home when he took the case. He didn't have much hope Maude hadn't read the inscription, but he'd decided on a good lie to tell her if he needed to.

Although Maude didn't have the watch with her, she did admit to "borrowing" it. And she made it clear she'd read the back too. Luckily for him, Maude was as trusting as she was larcenous and she believed the story he spun her. He made arrangements to pick up the watch from her later in the day and headed for the Chapman ranch.

A good while later, long enough for him to be hot, sweaty, and tired, Max stared at a large tin shack located on the far reaches of the Chapmans' land. The sight of it perked him up as quickly as a cold beer at the gates of hell. "Hot damn! Paydirt," he said softly. A halfway house if he'd ever seen one. The trail he'd followed that morning hadn't been substantially different than any of the others he'd traced to a dead end, but his instincts had told him this was the one. And he'd been right.

He approached it carefully, though it was clearly deserted. It hadn't rained in weeks. Besides footprints, he could see multiple tire tracks surrounding the building. From the looks of them he thought it likely they were truck tires. Pushing open the door, he recoiled as the stench hit his nostrils. Hell, a slaughterhouse smelled better than this place, he thought, disgusted. Obviously, no one had bothered with a privy. They'd packed people in there like animals, waiting to be taken to another location, no doubt with conditions mirroring the miserable ones he saw now.

No way to judge the last time it had been used. No indication of exactly who had been there, either. Then he spied a piece of paper trampled into the dirt floor. Squatting down, he worked it loose. A photograph of a family. One of the immigrant's family, he assumed. They looked Asian. Chinese, maybe, like the murdered immigrant. Turning it over, he stared at the writing. Not Spanish. Lines and symbols. It could easily be Chinese, he decided. He turned it back over to study the picture. This was something to send to the captain to check out.

He took another look around outside, though he didn't really expect to find much, figuring he'd already used up his quota of luck that morning. As he tromped around he noticed something glinting under a cactus plant about ten yards away.

Crouching, he smoothed the dirt away from it. A brass casing. He couldn't tell what kind of gun it came from, other than it was a 9mm. Many law enforcement personnel used 9mm. semiautomatics. Not Gracie, though. She had a .357 Magnum, which didn't eject the casings. Deputy Leroy Dunn, however, carried a 9mm. A Glock semiautomatic.

Carefully, Max used a plastic bag to pick the casing up, then placed it in another bag and zipped the bag shut. This discovery didn't prove that Dunn had been there, but it sure as hell had Max's suspicions vibrating at full load.

Another piece of the puzzle to send the captain. Finally, something useful.

Gracie had been trying to catch up on paperwork all morning, but thanks to certain people her concentration was shot. First, of course, there was Max. Probably hadn't been the brightest thing she'd ever done, telling him she loved him. Still, she didn't regret it. She wasn't sure why, but she thought Max needed to know that somebody loved him. She had an idea he hadn't heard those words nearly often enough.

Why was he so determined to leave, so dead set on not getting involved with her? His marriage was the obvious answer, the wife he claimed not to have loved. Max was running, that was clear, but what was he running from?

Sighing, she set her pen on the desk and shoved her hands through her hair. Maybe she was dreaming and he just plain didn't care that much about her. Except that wasn't what it felt like. Max made her feel that she was important to him, that she meant something to him, beyond the obvious pleasure he took from the sex. Being the object of a man's sexual desire was a new experience for her and one she found she liked, a lot. But she wanted more. Now how did she convince Max that he wanted more too?

Frustrated, she shoved her chair back and paced to the window. The small courtyard outside boasted a skimpy patch of grass around a live oak tree. Sometimes, in the spring or fall, she'd take her lunch out there and eat on the wrought-iron bench. It being the end of July, though, the grass looked burned and parched. Hot as Hell, she thought, smiling. The smile faded when she caught a glimpse of Leroy Dunn walking along the sidewalk toward the front of the building.

Things were strained between Gracie and her deputy. She had tried, without a lick of progress, to talk to him the night before when he took over for her. All he'd said was, "It's not your business, Sheriff. This is between Connie and me." And he hadn't budged from that position. Knowing him as she did, she doubted he would.

And dang it, he was right. She had no call to interfere, no matter what she suspected. Not unless Connie pressed charges and made it the law's business.

A knock interrupted her reverie. Leroy stuck his head inside the room. She wondered if his ears were burning or if that only applied when you talked out loud about someone. "Need to get to the file cabinet, Sheriff."

She waved him in and returned to her desk.

"Sheriff," he said in an odd tone a few moments later, "can you come over here?"

Mystified, she did. He'd opened one of the manila folders and laid it out on top of the other files. A letter lay on top of that, partially covering the other papers. "What's this?" she asked.

"A letter."

"I can see that, Leroy," she said, striving for patience.

"It's written in some kind of foreign language." His grave tone implied an importance she didn't quite get.

She looked down at the paper again. "Yep. Obviously not Spanish, though." Lines and symbols—Wait a minute, she thought. It looked like the markings on the Chinese food items she often got from the grocery store.

The murdered Chinese immigrant. Could it have something to do with him? If the writing *was* Chinese, then it sure seemed likely.

"But what's it doing in my dogfight file?" she wondered aloud.

"You didn't put it there?"

Puzzled, she asked, "Now why would I do that?"

"I thought—never mind," he said hastily when she frowned at him.

"What did you think, Leroy? You planning to get to the point anytime this century or are we just going to mosey around it?"

"Uh . . ." He hesitated, then gestured at the letter and asked, "What are you going to do with this?"

"Send a copy of it to Border Patrol, naturally. The only case I can think of that it might be connected to is that murdered immigrant—the Chinese illegal." She picked up the letter and inspected it more closely. "Border Patrol will be able to tell us if it's written in Chinese or Mandarin or whatever it is they speak over there. That should give us a good clue of where this"—she waved the letter—"belongs."

Leroy was staring at her like she'd lost her mind. "Do you think that's—?" He paused. "Wise?"

"Have a seat, Leroy." Gracie set the letter down and walked to her chair behind her desk, leaving the file drawer open. Her forearms on the desk, she leaned forward and pinned him with her gaze. "You'd better explain what the holy heck you're implying, Leroy. Otherwise I might get insulted. Is that what you're meaning to do?"

He looked worried. Concerned. "Sheriff, we both know you've got nothing to hide, but Border Patrol might not see it that way. Aren't they going to wonder why you didn't send this letter to them when you found the murdered man?"

"Why would they? You know as well as I do that man didn't have a scrap of paper on him. You watched me search him."

"Yes, ma'am, I did. And that's what I'll tell anybody who asks."

Shoving her chair back with a harsh scrape, Gracie stood. "Did you or did you not watch me search the body?"

"Well . . ." He shrugged. "Sure I did. It's just that the crowd was rambunctious and I was having a time dealing with them. The truth of the matter is, I didn't have my eyes on you the whole time."

Meaning she had had plenty of chance to palm the letter. But why would she? She couldn't think of a reason, unless she was involved in the murder. Her gaze locked with his.

"But no one besides you and me needs to know that," he added.

Shock held her still. He believed she was involved in that immigrant's murder. Why? Did he think she was a part of the smuggling ring?

"Don't worry, Sheriff," he said when she didn't speak. "I know where my loyalty lies."

Her temper fired like a bottle rocket on the Fourth of July. Three strides took her around her desk to stand over him. "Are you calling my integrity into question here?"

"No, ma'am," he said, solemn and sincere. "All I'm saying is the Border Patrol might see things different."

Hands fisted on her hips, she narrowed her eyes as she glared down at him. "Don't do me any favors, Leroy. Anybody asks, you tell them the truth."

The deputy stood, shaking his head in admiration. "You're a cool one, Sheriff. Just like your daddy before you."

Gracie stared at the door after he left. Just like her daddy? What the heck was that supposed to mean?

She thought about it the rest of the morning, replaying the scene with Leroy in her mind. The deputy believed she'd hidden that letter, that was plain. Who would ever have looked for it in a file about illegal dogfights? Besides that, she was the only person who ever looked at that particular file anyway.

So, she was under suspicion, at least by her deputy, of being involved with the illegal immigrant smuggling ring. Did Border Patrol suspect her too? If they didn't, they sure as heck would after they got that letter.

Or maybe . . . Maybe Leroy was setting her up. Playing the loyal deputy and all the while waiting to stab her in the back? Come to think of it, Leroy had found that letter just a little too easily to suit Gracie. He'd just *happened* to pull the dogfight file out while he was looking for another file. Mighty coincidental, she thought.

Could be *he* was involved in the smuggling ring. The longer she thought about it, the more certain she became that this was Leroy's way of focusing suspicion on her instead of himself. After all, who was more likely to be believed—Leroy Dunn, who didn't have a blemish on his name, or Grace O'Malley, daughter of the sheriff accused of taking bribes. A man many still believed had been guilty. Like father like daughter, she thought grimly.

Problem was, it didn't matter. She had no choice but to give Border Patrol the letter. If it could possibly help solve a murder, and she strongly suspected it could, then she had to send it to them.

Leroy's involvement in the smuggling ring would explain a lot of things. That inheritance of his, for one thing. And it made sense taken with what she'd overheard Connie say. "You wouldn't dare," Connie had told Leroy. "Not with what I know."

Exactly what did Connie know?

Questions, that was all she had. Not a single answer. She picked up the letter, taking it with her to the booking desk. She'd have an answer to at least one of her questions soon, she thought, feeding it into the fax machine. Then she'd tackle Connie. And Deputy Leroy Dunn.

She was hunting and pecking a letter at the old typewriter when Maude came in, all atwitter about something.

"Oh, Gracie, I'm so glad you're here instead of that deputy of yours." Her pale blue eyes earnest, her expression mildly outraged, she perched on the edge of the aluminum chair in front of Gracie's desk. "He was really quite rude, yes, positively rude to me the last time I—the last time— Well, when that dear boy missed his wallet."

Gracie suppressed a grin, envisioning Maude reading Leroy a lesson in manners as he tried to arrest her. Leroy had no patience with the postmistress. "What can I do for you, Maude?"

"It was just so shiny and pretty, you see," Maude told her sincerely. "I tried to resist it, really I did."

"What is it this time?" Didn't sound like a wallet. Gracie tried to think if she'd heard of anything going missing lately.

"He asked for it back so nicely too. But Sister's waiting for me and I can't disappoint her. So I thought of you."

While accustomed to following Maude's convoluted logic, Gracie still couldn't make sense of this one. "You've lost me, Maude. What do you want me to do?"

Producing something from the depths of her battered purse, Maude said, "I want you to give this back to that dear boy. The one you were kissing in the diner yesterday."

Gracie flushed scarlet, not knowing how to respond to that. Ignoring it was easiest, she decided. "You took something of Max's again?"

"Borrowed, my dear," Maude said reprovingly. "Merely borrowed it." She placed a watch in Gracie's hand. "You'll see that he gets it, then?" A little overwhelmed, Gracie nodded. "Poor thing," Maude continued. "If I'd known it belonged to his dead brother, I do believe I might have resisted it. He was killed in the line of duty, you know."

Gracie knew no such thing. In fact, she hadn't thought Max had any siblings. Maude turned the watch over and pointed at the back. "Isn't that the saddest thing you've ever heard?" Sighing, she wiped a tear away and left.

Gracie stared at the gold watch in her hands, her heart plummeting to her toes. The inscription danced before her eyes in sickeningly clear letters: *To Ranger Ridell. June 1993.*

ELEVEN

Early that evening, Max returned from a sixty-mile round-trip to an overnight delivery service. He'd used them to send the casing and picture to his captain. No way did he want to risk Maude getting a gander at the captain's address. Bad enough that she'd seen the watch and he'd had to make up a lie about that.

He'd only been back a few minutes when someone knocked on his door. Opening it, he saw Gracie standing on the threshold, unsmiling, as serious as he'd yet seen her. The flash of pleasure he felt nose-dived at her expression. When he bent to kiss her and she deliberately turned her cheek, he knew something bad had happened.

"I was just about to call you," he said, as she stepped past him without speaking.

She stood looking down at a box full of water

samples. "Guess you'll be finishing up here pretty soon."

A shiver of foreboding crawled up his spine. "Depends. I've still got quite a bit left to do." Like figure out a way to catch Dunn in the act of either transporting illegal immigrants or aiding and abetting their transportation. "Have you got something on your mind, Gracie? You're acting kind of strange."

"Am I?" Leaning back against the scarred dresser, she crossed her ankles and took her hat off, setting it beside her. "Now I wonder why that would be."

Maybe it was her eyes, he thought. Those cold, expressionless eyes. Not warm brown and sparkling with life, like they usually were. The flat, level voice didn't sound like her, either. "I'm not clairvoyant. Tell me what's going on."

She said nothing, fixing him with a penetrating stare for a moment longer. He knew exactly how her suspects felt, and fought the urge to squirm. When she finally did speak, her voice was devoid of inflection. "Maude came to see me this afternoon. Seems her magic fingers have been at it again. Except this time she shanghaied a watch."

His watch. Oh, God, Maude had given it to Gracie. He should have known she would, nothing was more likely. Had Gracie believed the story he'd spun Maude? Somehow, looking at her right now, he didn't think so.

"A real special type watch too," she continued,

pulling it from her pocket. She looked at it, then flipped it over to glance at the back. Her face remained expressionless, as bland and blank as he'd ever seen it. "Maude said it belonged to your brother." She met his eyes. "Your dead brother. Funny how you never mentioned him." Tossing him the wristwatch, she watched him catch it. His stomach rolled, and he wondered how he could have been so unbelievably stupid.

He didn't need to look at the inscription to know what it read. Nevertheless he did. *To Ranger Ridell. June 1993.* His gaze lifted to meet her icy, steady one.

"You've been playing a mighty deep game, haven't you, Ranger Ridell?"

Dammit! It would have been so simple to leave the watch at home, but he hadn't even thought of it. And he should have. It was a mistake more suited to a rookie than a seasoned Texas Ranger. His only excuse was that normally the Rangers didn't work undercover and this was his first assignment of that nature. It was a miracle in itself that Gracie hadn't read the inscription the first time she busted him. Even that hadn't forewarned him. "Gracie, I can explain."

Folding her arms across her chest, she nodded. "Oh, I expect you can. Ought to be right interesting too. I'm all atwitter waitin' to hear." Her drawl became more pronounced by the second, aided by the stinging sarcasm of her words. "Must be pretty darned important, I figure. What with the EPA covering for you and all. Yep." She tapped a finger to her forehead in a mocking salute. "Those Rangers sure do know how to run a quiet investigation."

"How did you find out?"

She rolled her shoulder. "It wasn't hard. No record of that brother of yours for one thing. Or any Ridell in recent years. They must've flagged your file and buried it deep for the time being. 'Course, I didn't really need confirmation, I knew when I saw the watch. You never have struck me as a biologist."

She pushed away from the dresser and stood up straight, planting her feet apart, her eyes boring into his. Her tone changed, sharpening and losing the drawling sarcasm. "Is it the bribes? Do you think I'm taking money like they accused my father of doing?"

He shook his head, wanting to offer at least one small consolation. "This has nothing to do with your father or his case."

"But you are investigating me. An undercover investigation."

"Of the sheriff's office," he admitted.

"What brought the Rangers into it? What are you looking for?"

There was no point keeping anything back now. He owed her what he knew. "We were given information which led us to suspect that either the Bandido County sheriff's department or the Border Patrol is heavily involved with an illegal alien smuggling ring. The one suspected of bringing Chinese and Pakistanis into the country by the cartload, routing them through Mexico."

"Well now, I feel a whole lot better," she said sarcastically. "At least somebody else is under suspicion too."

Now wasn't the time to tell her the Border Patrol had been all but ruled out. "I know you're angry. Hurt. You have every reason to—"

"Angry works," she interrupted, her voice as biting as a blue norther wind. "But I can think of a few more words that fit like hot lead in a bullet mold. Try betrayed. Roll your tongue around that one, Ranger Rii-dell. Or stupid. Dumber than dirt. Naive's a good one too."

"Gracie, I couldn't tell you. It's my job."

Her eyebrows shot up. "Is that a fact? Your job description calls for sleeping with the woman you're investigating?" She shook her head. "Mighty interesting job you got there. Must be some newfangled city method. Nothing like what I learned when I went to the academy. 'Course I'm just a no-account podunk county sheriff. Not a big, bad Texas Ranger like you."

He flushed, wishing he could offer an excuse, but there was none. "I know I shouldn't have gotten involved with you, but you were—I . . ." He wanted her, he thought. And hadn't been able to resist her.

"You saw an easy conquest and you took it,"

she said. "And I'll admit I made it even simpler, falling for you like a house of cards."

"No! Hell, Gracie, it wasn't like that. You know it wasn't."

"Do I?"

The phone rang. Max cursed viciously, making no move to answer it. Mercifully, the noise stopped after the sixth ring.

"I know what it was like for me," she said, "and now I'm clear on what it was for you."

Until that moment he'd seen her anger, but now he saw her pain. She'd told him she loved him, been open and honest with him, and he'd rewarded her with lies. "No you're not, dammit. If you'll—"

The phone rang again. Rather than let the intrusive jangle continue, Max grabbed it. "Ridell," he snapped.

"We just received some information you'll be interested in," his captain said.

God, now now, he thought, closing his eyes briefly. "Give me a minute," he told him. Covering the mouthpiece, he spoke to Gracie. "This is my captain. Will you wait so we can finish talking?"

She stared at him for a moment, then shrugged.

"All right," Max said into the phone. "Go ahead."

"Are you alone? Do you need to call me back?"

"No, go ahead."

"Border Patrol intercepted a transmission. Sounded like something big is going down next Tuesday. That's five days from now. We don't know where, though, just—"

"Don't worry about that. I know where," Max interrupted. "I located the halfway house today. I overnighted some evidence to you, but even without confirmation I'm ninety-nine-percent certain this is the place."

"Good work. Damn good work." He sounded pleased and a little relieved. "We'll set up the bust, then. Are you still liking the deputy for it?"

"More than ever."

"I've got to tell you, Ridell, our man with Border Patrol says they're making noises about the sheriff. Seems she faxed them a letter today that in all likelihood belonged to the murdered Chinese immigrant. They're very curious to know why it's just now coming to light. Claims she only discovered it today. Her deputy backed up her story when questioned, but he left a good bit open to conjecture."

Max bet he had. He could see Dunn's knife sticking out of Gracie's back. Along with the one she must feel he'd put there. "I'll check it out."

"You'd better." He waited a moment, and Max knew he wasn't finished. "How close to this situation are you, Ridell? I'm wondering if you're as objective as you should be."

Objective? He nearly laughed. Hell, no, he

wasn't objective. "Don't worry, Captain, I'll do my job." And that meant nailing Dunn's hide to the wall. Max was going to get a lot of pleasure from that, especially if, as he suspected, Dunn really was trying to finger Gracie.

Gracie didn't say a word as he hung up, just stood a few feet away looking at him like he was lower than a snake's underbelly. And he was. He'd known what he was doing was wrong, but he'd wanted her, wanted what she offered, and he'd taken it without thought to the consequences. The sex had been great, but that hadn't drawn him so much as the understanding, the acceptance, he found with her. The love, dammit.

"I never thought it was you," he said. "Not once I met you and got to know you."

"So that made it all right to sleep with me?"

"Dammit, Gracie, the investigation has nothing to do with our relationship."

"We didn't have a relationship, Max. We had sex. And now that's over." She strode to the door and would have been out it if he hadn't grabbed her arm to halt her.

"Wait. There's something you need to know. I think Dunn is setting you up."

"Now there's a news flash. Thanks, but I've already figured that out."

"You're under suspicion because of a letter you faxed Border Patrol. You need help. Let me help."

"I'd sooner trust a rattler." She looked him in

the eye and added, "But I already did that, didn't I?"

Telling Max off should have made her feel better, but after she left his room Gracie felt nothing except drained. She got into the patrol car and slumped in the seat, too tired to even turn it on. How could she have been so blind? she asked herself. And gullible. Ordinarily she wasn't a gullible person, but when she got taken in, she did it big time.

How could she have fallen in love with him? A fake, through and through. She wanted him gone, out of her life, out of her sight. And if he left, if she never saw that killer smile of his again or those beautiful blue eyes, never felt his arms around her again, how would she feel? Empty, she thought. Cold. Tears stung her eyes, though she fought them back. Even knowing him for a liar she was still in love with him. Talk about winning the prize for hopeless.

Well, she might be a fool, but she wouldn't sit around and do nothing but cry. Intending to wring the truth about Leroy Dunn out of Connie, she picked up her cell phone to track her friend down. Connie might not know everything Leroy was up to, but she knew something, and Gracie planned to find out what. The quickest way to clear her own name would be to bust that smuggling ring. And if Leroy Dunn *was* involved, then she meant to be the one to bring him down.

Leroy's part in all of it bothered her. After all, she'd given him chance after chance because she'd believed in his loyalty. Or tried to believe, anyway, because in her heart she'd never trusted him completely. Something about him had never rung true.

But Max . . . No, she wasn't going to think about him again. Not now, when she could be doing something useful. She'd think about him later, when the night closed in on her and she wouldn't be able to keep her mind off him.

Though she called everywhere, she couldn't track Connie down. Her friend wasn't at her house or the Chapmans'. Neither her mother nor sister had seen her. She was bound to be at Leroy's, Gracie realized. The one place she wasn't about to go looking for her.

The night, miserable enough to begin with, took a downward swing, starting with a one A.M. call, and ending with another around four-thirty. Every time she managed to fall asleep, the phone woke her up until she gave up and went to the office.

As she was leaving to get some breakfast at the diner, the phone rang one more time. It was Border Patrol. They confirmed that the letter she'd faxed was written in Chinese and requested an interview with her. They weren't coming over to talk about the weather, she knew. No, she was definitely a suspect.

"We need to talk," she told Connie when she arrived at the diner, relieved to see her friend at work. She'd been a little afraid Connie might not show up at all.

"Later," Connie said, leaving her a cup of coffee and hoisting her fully loaded tray again. "You know this is our busiest time."

"Yeah, I know. I'll wait." Thanks to the phone call she had hit rush hour, but Gracie didn't trust Connie not to disappear again as soon as she turned her back.

Frustrated as a woodpecker in a petrified forest, it didn't help that everyone who saw her wanted to know more about her "new beau" or that "dear boy" as Maude had taken to calling Max. Gracie thought she'd get lockjaw from biting her tongue, and her cheekbones ached from the phony smile she plastered on her face.

Finally, she couldn't stand it any longer. She rose, determined to drag Connie out of there by her hair if she had to. She stalked over to the counter and set her cup down with a sharp clatter. "Connie May, I'd appreciate it if you'd come with me to my office."

Connie slapped her hands on her hips and stared at her, smart-alecky as a kid sent to the principal's office. "You sound like you're bringing me in for questioning."

That did it. Nearly every eye and ear in the place were trained on the two of them now.

"If that's what it takes," Gracie said through gritted teeth, "then that's what I'll do. Don't push me any further on this, Connie."

They stared at each other, neither one budging an inch.

A thunderous, roaring boom split the air. The ground shook, trembling beneath their feet. Gracie whipped around and stared at the vibrating window, heard a rattle of dishes and then a second, even louder explosion.

She was the first one out the door.

TWELVE

The air stank of burnt rubber and scorched metal, with gas fumes so strong, they choked her. A black-and-gray mushroom cloud of smoke billowed up from behind the motel. Gracie ran toward it, still with no idea what had caused the horrendous sound or what she would find when she got there. Breathing heavily, coughing from the fumes, she reached the parking lot. The sight before her stole what was left of her breath and stopped her heartbeat.

She froze, staring in blank horror at the burning truck. *Max's truck. Oh, my God, it's Max's truck.* It was in front of his room, it had to be his. The flames prevented her from getting near enough to see inside it, but she knew with mind-numbing certainty that no one in the truck could have survived that explosion. Her heart choked, despair gripping it with frozen fingers.

Stunned, heartsick, she glanced wildly around for a sign of Max, praying he hadn't been in the truck. His motel room door was open. Hope kicked in as she ran inside the room. He lay crumpled on the floor beside the bed amidst a field of broken glass. Throwing herself on her knees beside him, she felt for a pulse and saw his eyelids flutter. He groaned and stirred, his eyes opening but with a blank, dazed expression filling them. His pulse beat slow and steady, warm and alive beneath her fingers. On a long, shaky sigh, she let out a breath she hadn't realized she was holding.

Max gazed at her, blinked, and groaned. "Gracie?" he said hoarsely.

"Don't move. You're hurt," she said, thanking God he was alive. Jerking her radio from her belt loop, she keyed the mike with shaking fingers. "There's been an explosion at the motel. Page the fire department and get EMS over here right away." She spoke to Cheryl more sharply than she ever had before. "Send me some backup too. I've got at least one injury, a burning truck in the parking lot, and I don't know what all damage to the motel."

"Oh, my God!" a voice said from across the room. Gracie glanced at Connie standing in the doorway, a hand clapped over her mouth in horror. "Is he—?"

"Alive," Gracie said, "but I don't know how badly he's hurt. Where's Bud?"

"Right here, Sheriff," the owner said. "Soon's I heard the boom, I came a-runnin'."

Max groaned again and shifted restlessly.

"Be still," Gracie told him, laying her hand on him for emphasis. "Anybody else hurt?" she asked Bud. He shook his head, and she continued. "Are the surrounding rooms occupied?" Those were the ones most likely to have someone injured inside them.

"Vacant. Good thing too. That explosion blew out the windows of four or five rooms. What in tarnation happened?"

"I don't know." A siren wailed nearby. Gracie silently blessed the volunteer fire department, knowing they'd be there in minutes. Joe, the paramedic with EMS, she wasn't so sure about. "Bud, you can go meet the fire department. Connie, see if Leroy or one of the reserves has gotten here yet. I'm going to stay with Max until the paramedic gets here."

They both left, though she practically had to push Connie out the door. Wanting to grab hold of Max and hug him tight, she instead lay a hand on his forehead.

Brushing her hand aside, he struggled to sit, still looking confused, though not as much as he had at first. "What . . . what happened?"

"You've been hurt," she repeated. "EMS is coming. Stay there, they'll be here in a minute." At least, she hoped they would.

Max ignored her, grimacing as he sat up. "I'm fine. I don't need a paramedic."

"Yes you do." She reached for him again, her fingers tracing a bump on the side of his head, wringing another groan from him. "I think this is your problem."

"Must have hit my head on the way down," he said.

"You were unconscious when I got here. You could have a concussion."

"No, I was just dazed, that's all." He put his hand to the bump on his head and cursed. "My head hurts like the devil, though. What happened here?"

Since she couldn't think of an easy way to break it to him, she just told him. "Your truck blew up."

Dropping his hand, he stared at her. "My . . . Did you say my truck blew up?"

She nodded and rose, thankful he couldn't know how fast her heart was racing and how scared she'd been when she first saw his truck. "The firemen are here. I'm going out to talk to them while they try to put out that fire. And I want to make sure Bud didn't miss anybody."

"I'm coming with you," he said grimly, and got to his feet. "How in the hell did my truck blow up?"

"I don't know. All I know is it did."

They stepped outside to an atmosphere black with smoke, heavy with fumes, and earsplitting with the wail of sirens. Gracie knew people were running around yelling, or standing in small groups watching, but her gaze was drawn relentlessly to the burned twist of metal that had once been Max's truck. Though the firehose aimed full force at it, flames licked up through the heavy stream of water. Max could have been in that fire. Closing her eyes, she fought back a wave of nausea.

"What the holy hell could have done this?" Max asked. He turned to her, their gazes meeting as he added slowly, "Or maybe I should say *who*."

She could only shake her head. "I don't know. I just . . . don't know."

A couple of hours later Max waited for Gracie in her office. His head hurt like a son of a bitch, and the cuts from flying glass still stung. Groaning, he closed his eyes and put it in his hands. He didn't have time for a headache, he needed to think.

They still didn't know much, but he was convinced that his truck's destruction was no accident. He wondered if the ranchers were behind it. It seemed like a major escalation of the grief they'd been giving him though. Being shot at, having dogs sicced on him, or having his tires slashed didn't exactly compare to being blown to smithereens. Only pure luck, forgetting his gun and going back to the room to get it, had saved him.

"You should have gone to the hospital," Gracie said as she walked in.

He raised his head and glanced at her. Her face was smudged, her uniform filthy with soot and blood. At the sight of the blood, he frowned. "Are you hurt? Was someone else hurt? Why is there blood on your uniform?"

She stopped beside his chair and showed him a bandaged hand. "Cut myself on the glass."

He took her hand and turned it over to look at it more closely. Gauze covered the pad of her thumb. "I hurt you again," he murmured, rubbing his thumb over her palm.

Jerking her hand away, she shrugged it off. "It's nothing. You're the one who's hurt."

"The paramedic said it wasn't a concussion. I never lost consciousness."

"Don't forget I know that paramedic," she said, tossing some papers on her desk. "Caesar's better trained than he is. I wish you'd let them take you to the county hospital and give you a CAT scan."

She still cared about him. He could see it in her anxious eyes, hear it in the worried tone of her voice. The tightness in his chest eased. It surprised him and even more, it scared him, that what she felt mattered so much to him. "Thanks."

"For what?" she asked.

"For caring."

Characteristically, she didn't try to brush it aside. Her eyes darkened as she looked at him. She didn't seem happy. "I can't change my feelings overnight. I wish I could."

"I'm glad you haven't." What was wrong with him? That blast had shaken him more than he'd thought. He had no business saying something like that to her.

"A bomb expert from El Paso is on his way," she said at length, not acknowledging his last comment.

Max latched on to the change of subject like a lifeline. "I don't need a bomb expert to tell me somebody blew up my truck. There was nothing wrong with that truck. Nothing of that magnitude, anyway."

"We won't know for sure until we've heard from the experts. Right now I think you should let me take you to my place."

"I'm not leaving until I know something."

"That won't be for hours yet. You can talk more freely from my house. I'm sure there are people you need to call."

His captain, for one. But he wanted to discuss some things with Gracie before he called him. She was looking at him expectantly. Talk more freely, she'd said. Did she have a reason for not wanting to discuss the case at her office? "All right. Let's go."

He followed her out to the patrol car, keeping

silent while she cranked the engine and started to drive.

"I've been thinking about this," she said without preamble. "Your truck didn't blow up by itself, but I don't believe it's the ranchers. It's not like them to be so sneaky and underhanded. If they wanted to get rid of you, they'd be a lot more likely to shoot you than to plant a bomb."

"I agree. I don't think the ranchers did it either." Partly because he knew more than she did. "There's something you should know, Gracie. Border Patrol has been essentially eliminated as a suspect in the case."

Her hands tightened on the steering wheel. "Which means my office is involved. Me or Leroy, is that it?"

"You're not a suspect, Gracie. At least as far as I'm concerned." She didn't answer, but he could see her grip loosen on the wheel. "So that means it's Dunn," he continued. "But what would make him take such a step?"

"Your cover might have been blown. The story you spun Maude has been making the rounds. Could be Leroy heard it and put two and two together." She cast him a sideways glance. "He's not as dumb as he seems, either."

Max flushed. "I never thought you were dumb. Hell, I've been having to tap-dance just to keep one step ahead of you, and I haven't done a very good job of it."

She ignored that and continued in the earlier

vein. "But like you said, what would make Leroy so anxious to get rid of you? Killing you seems pretty drastic, even if he was positive you were a Ranger."

"There's going to be a big load of illegals coming through on Tuesday. He'd want me gone before that. And I don't think killing one Ranger is all that drastic considering the amount of money we're talking. Especially since my death could easily be blamed on the ranchers."

"Or me."

"Or you," he was forced to agree. "I hadn't thought of that but you're right." If she were under suspicion for smuggling, she could be under suspicion for his murder as well once his identity became known. "This development makes it even more likely that our information is good."

"Gee, that's a relief," she said sarcastically. "And all it took was a near fatal accident."

As they pulled up to the house Max noticed a red Ford Escort and saw Connie waiting on the porch. "Looks like you've got company."

"Looks like." Gracie turned into the drive and killed the engine. "I want in on the sting," she said, putting her hand on his arm to restrain him. "Leroy Dunn is my deputy, and it's my office he's destroying. My office and my career."

"Too dangerous." He understood her desire, but his gut instinct told him to keep Gracie out of it.

"I have a right to be there, Max. And it's no

more dangerous for me than it is for you or any other officer."

She was right, but he didn't want that danger to touch her. They stared at each other, and he knew he'd lose this battle. She meant to go, and she would. The captain was going to give him a lot of grief when he broached the subject with him. "All right," he finally said. "But I think it's a mistake. I'll find out the details when I talk to the captain. He and Border Patrol are setting it up."

She nodded and opened her door. "I'll let you in so you can get started. I need to talk to Connie alone."

Gracie led her friend to the barn on the pretext of helping her with the animals. She didn't speak and for once, neither did Connie. What had brought her there? she wondered. Had she finally decided to tell her about Leroy? Maybe that explosion had knocked some sense into that stubborn red head of hers.

Even if it hadn't, Gracie was fed up with waiting and she meant to get some answers. Max's life was on the line.

Connie was acting strange, all right. Look at her now, Gracie thought. Caesar stuck his nose up under her skirt and all she did was halfheartedly shove him away. Usually she yelled at him and pitched a fit.

"Gracie, I—I've got some things to tell you, and you're not going to be very happy with me."

Gracie took a seat on a bale of hay, and Connie sat beside her. "I'm not here to judge you. Just talk to me."

"I think Leroy blew up Max's truck," she blurted out. "Or if he didn't, he knows who did."

Even though she'd suspected him, hearing Connie's statement jarred Gracie. "Why do you think that?"

"Something I heard. Late last night, I was . . . I was with Leroy last night." She met Gracie's steady gaze, shame in her own.

"I figured as much. I looked for you everywhere and couldn't find you. Go on."

"He was talking on the phone. He thought I was asleep, I guess. Or," she added, anger replacing shame, "too dumb to think anything even if I did hear it. But then this morning, when I saw that truck, and saw Max lying there—Oh, God, Gracie, I swear I didn't know it was that bad. I never imagined he meant to do something like that." The tears that had been threatening spilled down her cheeks.

Gracie did her level best to shove aside her own fears about Max being dead. Every time she thought of what could have happened, dread ripped through her. "What did you hear?"

Connie sniffled and wiped her eyes, composing herself enough to continue. "Leroy was arguing with someone over the phone. I got the idea they'd been going back and forth about something for a while. Finally he said, 'Don't worry, I'll teach him to mind his own business. Nosy EPA agents have to expect problems down here.' And he laughed when he called him an EPA agent. I knew he was talking about Max, but I swear to God, I never thought he'd—he'd try to hurt him.''

"Call it what it was, Connie May," Gracie said harshly. "Attempted murder. It's time you told me the whole story about Leroy and you. Like why you ever took up with him in the first place."

Connie was silent, pleating her skirt nervously before she finally spoke. "He was exciting." At Gracie's skeptical look, she said, "He is. You don't know what he's like when he's trying to impress you. I guess I was flattered. And all Reese ever talks about, all he cares about is that damned ranch."

"Reese has been working his tail off to make a go of it. For you as much as for him, Connie."

"It doesn't seem that way. All he ever does is pat me on the head, kiss my cheek, and say, 'Not now, honey. I've got work to do.' "

"So you had an affair with Leroy."

"Yes." Half shamed, half defiant, she continued. "And then once I did, Leroy started dropping hints that he knew something about the Chapmans that would ruin them. So if I wanted Reese not to get in trouble with the law, I'd better make Leroy happy. Of course, he threatened to tell Reese about us too."

"Why didn't you come to me?"

"It was a slow thing. It didn't happen all at once." She passed a hand over her forehead. "When I realized what I'd gotten into I was afraid to come to you, because of what he'd do to the Chapmans. He told me they were into something illegal, and I know how you feel about the law, Gracie. You'd never look the other way, and I was afraid for them. For Reese. Because I'd realized I still loved him and what an idiot I'd been. Leroy never told me what it was they were doing, but I thought he was hooked up with it too. He'd let things slip now and then that made me suspicious. And when we first started seeing each other, he'd spend loads of money on me. I was never sure where it came from."

"What about when he beat you up? You wouldn't trust me even after that?"

Connie stared at her. "He did that because I threatened to go to you with my suspicions about him. And because I wanted to call things off and he didn't."

"If you'd come to me sooner—"

"I messed up!" she shouted, springing to her feet. "I should've come to you. Better yet, I should never have taken up with Leroy in the first place. But I can't change that. I can't change it." She started crying again, all the fight draining out of her.

"No, I know." Gracie watched her cry, waiting patiently until she pulled herself together. She ached for Connie, but she also had to admit that Connie had brought a lot of the pain on herself by her behavior.

Finally Connie continued. "When Max's truck blew up, I knew I had to do something. No matter what happened to me, I knew I couldn't stand by and let Leroy—let him kill a man and say nothing."

"You did the right thing."

"A little late, don't you think? I've been doing the wrong thing for months. Reese will never forgive me. Never."

Gracie was afraid of that, too, but didn't want to add to her friend's misery. "You don't know that."

"He'll think I betrayed him, and he's right. Even you couldn't forgive betrayal."

Couldn't she? Gracie asked herself as she went to tell Max the news.

Max was winding up a frustrating call to his captain when Gracie came in. "It was Leroy," she said, after he hung up. "Ninety-nine-percent sure, anyway. Connie overheard a phone call." She filled him in on the details, none of which surprised him.

"It makes sense," he said. "The Chapmans, or one of them, almost have to be involved. There's no way to move that many people through their land without someone knowing it. And this gives me something to hand the captain about you to convince him to let you in on the sting."

"You told him?"

He'd had no choice. "Yeah, I told him." He frowned, remembering. "You're not a suspect, and I don't want him and Border Patrol thinking you are."

"What did he say?"

His head averted, Max didn't speak. After a moment, he turned his head and met her gaze. "He says I'm hung up on you and it's clouding my thinking."

Gracie gaped at him. Finally she asked, "Are you?"

Was he? Maybe he was, but he couldn't admit it. He shrugged and didn't answer. "It doesn't matter. I know damn good and well you're not involved in that ring."

"It matters to me."

Now wasn't a good time to be having this conversation. So why had he mentioned what the captain thought? Because his damn brains had been scrambled in that blast, that's why. His head pounded in agreement. He grimaced and rubbed his temples. "It doesn't matter because I'm not getting into that trap again." No matter what he might think he felt for Gracie, he wouldn't take the risk.

She walked out of the room. He thought she'd gotten angry and left the house, except she came back a minute later carrying aspirin and water. "Here, you look like your head hurts."

Damn, she disarmed him at every turn. He swallowed the pills and sat on the couch.

"What trap?" she asked, and sat beside him.

Nothing he said was likely to make a difference now. Except maybe if he explained she'd realize what a lucky break it would be for her when he left. So he told her the truth. "Love. Marriage. Duty. Especially duty."

"You're a Ranger. I wouldn't have thought you had a problem with duty."

"That's different. Law enforcement is what I want. It's a different kind of duty. Not the same at all as being forced to do the right thing."

Tilting her head, she considered him. "Doing the right thing. Like staying with your dying wife."

He met her brown eyes squarely. "Yeah, exactly like that."

"So you stayed with her out of duty, because it was the right thing to do."

"That's right."

"I never told you how my mother died, did I?" Confused by the non sequitur, he just looked at her. "She had ovarian cancer, Max, like your wife. My father and I were with her until the end. My father would have done anything to spare her that pain, but in the end all he could do was watch her die, and be there for her." She touched his arm and smiled gently. "Duty? Maybe. But I think a man has to love someone very much to stick with her through all that."

She rose and looked down at him. "I'm going back to work to see if the bomb expert's here yet. I'll call when I know anything."

Silently, he watched her go, wondering why she was crediting him with decent motives when she had every reason not to. At the door she paused. "I'd feel better if you stayed here tonight. You can use the guest room." Giving him no time to argue, she left.

Max stared at the doorway, amazed and shamed by Gracie's reaction. How could she give so freely? Offer her hospitality, her home, her understanding, to a man who'd done nothing but lie to her and hurt her?

She was a gift, he realized. A gift of love and generosity. He slumped against the back of the couch and closed his eyes. A gift he sure as hell didn't deserve.

THIRTEEN

At midnight Gracie admitted she wasn't going to sleep, got out of bed, and went to her bedroom window. Stupid of her to expect to sleep with temptation itself lying twenty feet away in her guest bedroom.

She wanted to go to Max. It wasn't smart, but her heart didn't care about smart. Her heart only cared that the man she loved lay sleeping in her guest bedroom and she wasn't with him. The only thing that held her back was the knowledge that she'd gone to Max both times before. This last time, if there was to be a last time, had to be his choice. He had to make the first move.

And she didn't think he would. For one thing, she'd all but told him to drop dead the other day at the motel. Still, she argued with herself, he had to know she'd forgiven him at least a little or she'd never have asked him to stay. The destruction of his truck, and the pure luck that he hadn't been in it, had brought everything into perspective for her. She loved him. She wanted him. And if she were offered the opportunity, she'd have him again, even if he left tomorrow. Memories would fuel a lot of lonely nights. A lifetime's worth.

The night air blew cool through the open window, raising goose bumps on her skin. As hot as Hell was, the nights were desert cool. Wearing only a cotton T-shirt, the same shirt she'd lent Max not long ago, she shivered and crossed her arms over her chest. Sighing, she leaned her head against the windowsill and watched the moonlight play over the barn, dapple the fields with moon glow.

"Gracie."

His deep, smoke-roughened voice came from the doorway. Her heart rate sped up even though she told herself he was probably only looking for more aspirin. Afraid if she saw him she'd throw herself at him again, she didn't turn around. "I'm here," she said, and waited.

He came to stand behind her. She sensed the heat from his body before she felt his hands touch her shoulders. "I couldn't stay away from you," he said. "I tried like hell, but I just couldn't do it."

"Are you talking about tonight? Or . . . before?"

"Both." He pulled her back against him, yet his hands stayed on her shoulders. His warm breath touched her ear, making her shiver with longing. "Every time I was around you I'd get in a little deeper. You were almost too good to be true, but you were real." He sounded bewildered. "It blew me away. I think you put a spell on me."

She had to laugh at that. "Oh, yeah, I'm a regular enchantress."

"You have no idea." He wrapped his arms around her at last. "I've never met anyone like you. That sounds like a line, but it's not. I've never met anyone more generous. More giving. More forgiving." He was quiet a moment, then said, "You've forgiven me, haven't you, Gracie? For lying to you. For hurting you."

Unable to speak over the lump in her throat, she nodded. Max was talking as if he loved her. She wondered if he realized it. She didn't think he did. "When I saw your truck today, when I thought what could have happened . . ." The memory made her shudder. "I couldn't hold on to the anger. Didn't want to hold on to it."

His lips touched her neck, his arms tightened around her. His deep voice was dark, quiet and still as the night. "I want to make love with you, Gracie. Now that you know who I am. Now that you know why I'm here and why I still have to leave when it's over. Now that there aren't any lies between us."

Her mind knew it was a mistake, but her heart and her body betrayed her. Her head rested against his shoulder and his neck, his bare chest and arms surrounded her with heat. She could feel the soft denim of his jeans against her bottom and the bite of the buttons of his fly against her back. The hard ridge of his erection pressed against her, too, letting her know how much he wanted her. She had no defense against him, against the need, both their needs, and she raised her arm to reach back and touch his cheek with her fingers.

"Say yes, Gracie," he whispered, and kissed her fingers. "Say yes."

She followed her heart. "Yes," she breathed, and turned her head to meet his kiss. He made love to her mouth, his lips moving so gently over hers, his tongue seeking hers out, meeting it and drawing it inside his own mouth with loving persuasion. It was a kiss so achingly tender that tears stung at her eyes.

The kiss went on until she thought she'd drown in it, drown in him, in the smell, the feel, the taste of him, and all the while he did nothing more than kiss her. When his lips left hers, he pressed hot, openmouthed kisses to her neck. She stirred and started to turn in his arms, but he murmured, "Wait," and stayed her.

His hands skimmed up her rib cage, each coming to rest beneath a cotton-covered breast. Her breathing quickened as she waited, her nipples tightening in anticipation. His fingers touched the sides of her breasts, retreated, touched again. Moaning, she raised her other arm to reach behind his neck, to dig her fingers into the silky strands of his hair. His palms grazed her nipples with a bare touch. Her breath hissed in, and he did it again.

"You're driving me crazy," she whispered.

He laughed softly. "Good. Because you drive me crazy too."

Still he kept the contact light, teasing her until her breasts ached with longing. His teeth closed on her neck, and his hands reached underneath her shirt, now stroking bare skin. "Touch me," she finally said, driven to ask or go insane.

"I am. Feel it." His finger circled her nipple, barely touching her.

"No, I mean really touch me," she said, and closed his hands over her naked breasts. He did what she asked, rubbing and fondling her breasts until she thought she'd climax from that alone. Then he raised the hem of her shirt, inch by inch, drew it over her head and started again.

He slid one hand down from her breast to glide over her panties, to feel the moisture between her legs and feed the fire raging inside her.

"Open your legs," he said hoarsely.

She widened her stance, and he slipped his hand inside her panties. He stroked his fingers over her for what seemed like hours, then cupped her and pulled her back against him even more tightly. He plunged his finger deep inside her and she shattered, crying out as he drove her over the crest.

"Now," she heard him say, the words coming dimly through a haze of desire. "I want you now,

Gracie. I need you now." His arms dropped away from her, and she sagged against him, felt him unfastening his jeans and pushing them off. Turning her around, he kissed her once, hard and fierce, then dragged her to the bed, falling onto it backward, pulling her on top of him.

Staring down at him, she felt strong, feminine, powerful. Her smile was slow as she reached across him to the drawer of her bedside table. Her breast grazed his mouth, and she gasped when his mouth clamped over her nipple. She managed to find what she was looking for and moved so her other breast taunted him, until he latched on and suckled her deeply.

He reached out to take the condom from her, but she shook her head and smiled wickedly. "No, I want to," she said. His hand dropped. He stared at her, then nodded. She took her time, partly because she wasn't at all sure what she was doing, and partly because she could tell she was driving him to the brink of madness and she reveled in it.

Oh, so slowly, she slid down over him, taking him little by little until he was embedded deep inside her. She threw back her head and groaned, heard his echoing groan as they began to rock together, faster and faster until they neared the end, dancing along the edge of rapture. Grasping her hips, he surged upward. He spilled inside her as her climax overtook her in a tremendous torrent of passion, pleasure . . . and love.

She collapsed on his chest, and they lay there

breathing heavily. She wanted to stay that way forever, but she knew forever would never happen. Finally, he shifted, and she raised up to look at him.

He stared into her eyes, so solemnly, she wondered what he could be thinking. "You're beautiful, Gracie," he said, and pulled her head down to kiss her lips.

She gave herself over to his kiss, and for the first time in her life, she felt beautiful.

Max spent the next morning watching Gracie work. Since they couldn't afford to confirm Dunn's suspicions by allowing Max to help with the investigation, he was still undercover. Restless, he got up to pace her office. There wasn't much he could do in that case, except wait for the sting to take place on Tuesday.

The bomb experts had verified his and Gracie's suspicions. A simple pipe bomb had been placed beneath the engine of his truck, set to explode a minute after ignition. If he hadn't forgotten his gun and gone back inside to get it, he'd have been blown into as many pieces as his pickup. Luck, pure stinking luck, had saved him. The pencil he was holding snapped in two. Somebody, by God, was going to pay.

Gracie and he went to the diner for lunch, but when they got into the patrol car afterward, she didn't head for the police station.

"Are you going to your place?" he asked, recognizing the route. "Why? We've still got work to do at your office."

"Nope." One corner of her mouth lifted as she cut him a shrewd glance. "*I've* got work to do. You're going home. Take a nap. Call your captain."

He frowned, curbing his irritation. "I don't need a nap. I'm fine, I told you that." She ignored him and kept driving. "Gracie, I don't need to go to your place. I can wait in your office while you work."

"No, you can't." She glanced at him again and smiled before turning her gaze back to the road.

"Of course I can. I was there all morning."

"Yep." She nodded. "And that's why you're going to my place this afternoon. Because I'm gonna strangle you if you ask me one more thing about my investigation of that bomb." Halting at a stop sign, she turned and looked him in the eye. "I know what I'm doing, you can't help me right now, and you're going to my place. Discussion's over."

She took off with Max gaping at her, unable to believe how she was overreacting. He didn't think he'd asked that many questions, but the set of her jaw told him he could forget any arguments. They rode the rest of the way in silence.

Damned stubborn woman, he thought a few minutes later as he watched her drive away from her house.

Much to his annoyance, he fell asleep on the couch. He had to admit he felt a lot better when he woke up. With nothing more pressing to do, he decided to cook dinner. A search through Gracie's cupboards and refrigerator revealed all the ingredients for chili. Luckily, chili was one of the few dishes he cooked well, so he set about making it.

While it was simmering, he poked around the house. It was a lot like Gracie. Warm, comforting, with unsuspected depths. Judging by the books she'd left lying open in various rooms, her reading tastes were widely varied. A legal thriller in the kitchen, science fiction in the living room, and a romance in her bedroom.

Her old-fashioned bedroom held a dark cherry four-poster, a matching dresser, and a chest of drawers. A freestanding oval mirror stood in the corner. A handmade quilt covered the bed with pillows spilling across it, thrown on in haste when she left that morning.

It had been a mistake, he realized, to come into her bedroom. Her scent surrounded him, and memories of the night before assailed him. The sight of her face flushed with passion, with love. The sound of her laughter. How she looked as she fell asleep in his arms, and how he felt when he held her through the night. The night before, he finally admitted, hadn't been solely about sex.

Dammit, he was falling in love with Gracie.

He'd been in love with Marla too. At first. Until he'd had to bury his dreams because of her expectations, her dreams. Because of duty. And then she'd gotten sick and duty had become an even heavier burden. Gracie believed he'd loved his wife in the end, but Gracie believed the best of everyone. It was one of her strengths, as well as one of her weaknesses, to believe like that.

He heard the back door slam and left the bedroom, thankful to have an excuse not to examine his feelings more closely. Falling in love would change nothing, he knew. Love brought duty along with it, and the burden of duty killed love— and dreams. At least, it had for him.

So he would leave when the job was over, and Gracie would find someone else, a man who deserved her.

She was standing at the stove tasting the chili when he walked into the kitchen. A wave of lust, and worse, longing, swept over him. What would it be like, he wondered, to come home to Gracie every night, or have her coming home to him? Could it be different with Gracie, or would it turn to ashes and bitterness, like it had before?

He couldn't take the risk.

She turned and saw him watching her from the doorway. "You make a mean chili," she said, smiling and gesturing at the pot with her spoon. "Does this mean you've forgiven me?"

How could he resist her? In spite of his decision, or perhaps because of it, he went to her.

They didn't have a future, but they had the here and now, and he would have her while he could.

He crossed the room. "Forgiven you for kicking me out of your office?" Taking the spoon from her, he tossed it on the counter. "I could be convinced." He pulled her into his arms and kissed her, then drew back to look at her. Her eyes were wide and smiling, her mouth curved in a cocky grin. "Have I ever told you how sexy you look in this uniform?" He kissed her collarbone and slid his hands up her torso.

She laughed, then sighed as his hands closed over her breasts. "No, but you can tell me now." Her arms were around his waist, her head thrown back to expose a luscious view of her neck.

"You look even sexier," he said, beginning to unfasten her buttons, "out of it."

"The animals—"

"Can wait." He finished with the shirt and started on her slacks.

"The chili—"

"Can simmer. Right now I'm more interested in the way you simmer when we make love."

Her eyes darkened, her arms tightened around his waist. "You're a mighty persuasive man, Max Ridell. I guess next thing I know you'll be talking your way into my bedroom."

"Later." He smiled wickedly. "The table's closer."

"The table?"

"Absolutely." He laid her out on it, leaned down, and kissed her.

"Much closer," she whispered, and put her arms around his neck.

The phone rang while Gracie was washing up after dinner. Bad news, she thought, glancing at the clock. A call this late never meant good news. She grabbed the receiver, nearly dropping it into the dishwater. "O'Malley."

"You're home," Connie said. "I thought—I thought you'd be gone, but you're home." Her voice was hoarse, agitated.

"Yep," Gracie said, drying her hands on a dish towel and wondering what had gotten into her friend this time. "What's up?"

"The Chapmans. I need your help, Gracie."

She'd been crying, was crying still, Gracie realized. "What's wrong? What happened? Did Reese find out about you and Leroy?"

"Just—just come to the Chapmans'."

Gracie could barely hear her. "I'll be there as soon as I can."

"No!" Connie shouted suddenly, her anguished voice coming out in a choked cry. "It's a—"

The line went dead.

FOURTEEN

"I heard the phone," Max said, walking into the kitchen. "Do you have to go out on a call?"

Gracie shook her head. "Not exactly. That was Connie. Calling from the Chapmans', I think." Briefly, she related the conversation, including how abruptly it had ended. Surely Reese hadn't . . . But even Reese had his limits, Gracie thought.

"I'm going over there," she told Max. "Don't wait up for me. No telling how long I'll be." Or what she'd find when she got there, she thought, picking up her gun belt. She turned to see Max frowning at her.

"I don't like it," he said. "There's something wrong about this."

Nodding, she fastened her belt at her waist. "There's a whole lot wrong. It's a mess, and I'm going to see what I can do to fix it."

He shook his head. "No, it's more than that. I've got a bad feeling about this. Don't go, Gracie." He put his hand on her arm as if to stop her.

Surprised, she looked at him. "You know I have to. It's my job, and besides that, Connie's my friend. I'll be fine."

He searched her face for a long moment. "Let me go with you."

"Max, you can't. This has nothing to do with the investigation, anyway."

"Maybe it does."

"And maybe you're overreacting." She raised her hand to his cheek and smiled. "You know, it's awful sweet of you to worry about me, but it's not necessary. I've got to go." She started to kiss his cheek, but he turned so she kissed his mouth instead.

"Be careful," he said gruffly.

"Count on it."

Driving off, Gracie wasn't as unconcerned as she'd let Max think. That phone call had been downright weird, especially how Connie had hung up on her—or had been cut off.

Her uneasiness grew when she reached the Chapman ranch house and saw that it was shut down for the night with only a porch light burning. She climbed the steps, glancing around and wondering why she felt like a knife was aimed between her shoulder blades. She rang the bell and waited.

Reese finally answered, barefoot, bare-chested,

wearing a pair of jeans, his hair mussed like he'd just gotten out of bed. "Gracie?" He scratched his head and stared at her. "Is something the matter?"

"Is Connie here?"

He rubbed his jaw and appeared to ponder the question before answering in his slow drawl. "No, she's been a little put out with me lately, I reckon."

"But—she called a while ago and asked me to come out to the ranch. I figured she'd be here."

Mystified, he shook his head. "Now I wonder why she'd do something like that? Haven't seen her in three, maybe four days."

Gracie stared at Reese, at his kind, bewildered face. He had no idea that anything was wrong. Connie hadn't told him, and obviously, neither had Leroy. So why had Connie called her out there?

"You think something's wrong, Gracie?" Reese continued, more anxious now that he was awake.

"No, no, I'm sure she's fine. But why don't you go make some calls and see if you can get hold of her, Reese. I'll take a look around, if you don't mind."

"Sure thing, Gracie. I'll get right on it."

She walked back to the patrol car, trying to figure out what in the world Connie was up to. Her hand on the door handle, she heard the crunch of gravel and started to turn. Something struck her temple hard. Blackness swallowed her as she crumpled to the ground.

Gracie came to with her head aching to beat Dixie, lying on a hard dirt floor trussed up tighter than a Thanksgiving turkey. Her hands were fastened behind her, cold metal handcuffs ringing her wrists. All she could tell from the dim light in the room was that she was in some kind of tin shack. A surge of nausea hit her, and she groaned. Leroy Dunn's face filled her vision.

"Look who's awake," he said, smiling nastily.

Good job, Gracie, she thought. Caught like a rookie in the simplest trap. It took her a minute before she could speak. "What did—what did you do to Connie?"

"If you had any sense you'd worry about your own hide, not Connie's."

"If you've hurt her—"

"You're in no position to make threats, Sheriff. But Connie's just fine. For now." Grasping her arm, he jerked her up, shoving her back against the wall.

Gracie shut her eyes, fighting another wave of nausea and dizziness as her head exploded with pain.

"You're even more of a pain in the butt than your old man was," she heard him say. "But I fixed him, and I can fix you too."

Her mind cleared as the pain receded to a

throbbing ache. "Fixed him," he'd said. All this time she'd thought Leroy had helped her father. Instead, he'd betrayed him. "You framed him for taking those bribes, didn't you? Why?"

Leroy shrugged. "It wasn't my fault. I didn't want to, but he forced me to. He was getting too close to the smuggling operation. We were just beginning then and couldn't afford anyone nosing around, least of all the sheriff."

"Why tell me now?" She thought she knew. She hoped she was wrong.

"You know why." He shot her a quick, uneasy glance.

"Humor me. Spell it out for me."

His expression was almost regretful as he looked down at her. "Because you're going to have to die, of course, along with that Ranger lover of yours."

Gracie heard a sound like a muffled scream, coming from inside the room. Connie, she thought, her heart beating faster. Oh, Lord, no. He'd brought Connie with him. "I don't know what you're talking about."

Leroy slapped her mouth, hard. Gracie's head snapped back; she tasted blood.

"Now look what you made me do." He straightened, giving her a stern look. "Sheriff, don't play that dumb-broad act with me, y'hear? Ridell is a Texas Ranger, and we both know it. Lie to me again and I'll have to get mean."

The pain was making it hard to concentrate,

but the adrenaline surge of fear helped sharpen her wits. "Leroy, think about what you're doing. You don't want to do this." She'd worked with this man for eighteen months. Could her instincts be so wrong? Leroy was a bully, a liar, a thief, but he wasn't a cold-blooded murderer. She couldn't believe that of him.

"Of course I don't *want* to," he said. "But you've given me no choice." He paced away from her, waving the gun. "If you hadn't hooked up with that Ranger he'd have believed you were the one involved and everything would have been fine. How was I to know they'd involve the Texas Rangers? And worse, that he'd fall for you?"

"You're not a murderer. Once you commit murder you'll cross a line that will drive you mad. I know you, Leroy, and you're not a killer."

"Yeah? Who do you think killed that immigrant?"

She caught his gaze and held it. "Not you. I imagine one of the coyotes did that."

As he stared back at her, she thought she saw a spark of something like regret in his eyes, but then it was gone. "Nice try, but you won't talk your way out of this one, Sheriff. I can't afford to let you live."

"You won't get away with it."

"Oh, I think I will." His high-pitched, nervous laughter grated on her already shredded nerves. "Long enough to make one last deal and get out, anyway. But don't worry, I'm not going to kill you. You and your lover are going to do each other in."

"Might be hard since I don't see him around."

"He'll be here." Leroy pulled out his cellular phone and punched in a number. "You're going to get him here."

"No."

He squatted down and put the gun barrel underneath her chin. The cold metal dug into her skin as he used it to tilt her head back. She could see the sweat beading on his forehead, see the desperation running wild in his eyes. He walked a tight edge of violence. It didn't inspire her with a lot of hope.

"You'll talk to him and tell him to come out here or I'll blow your fool head off."

Bile rose in her throat. She tasted fear along with the blood trickling from her split lip. He might not mean to kill her in cold blood, but he sure as heck could get upset and kill her anyhow. The gun pressed to her pulse felt real and deadly. "It doesn't matter what you do to me, I won't call him."

"Knowing you like I do, Sheriff, I kinda thought you'd take this attitude."

He rose and stepped aside. For the first time, Gracie could see directly across the room. Her heart plummeted, fear squeezing it in a harsh vise. Connie lay on the ground, her mouth gagged, hands behind her, feet bound with a rope. A lantern sat close by, and Gracie could see her eyes, see the raw terror shining in them. Gracie didn't blame her. She was scared nearly witless herself and she'd been trained for situations of this sort. Poor Connie was probably catatonic with fear.

Pure, hot fury bubbled in her veins, with nowhere to go. She was caught like a prairie dog in a rattler's sights. Leroy squatted beside her again and murmured, "How about you call Ranger Ridell or I blow *Connie's* head off? How about that, Sheriff?"

Her stomach heaved. She could take the chance with her life, but not with Connie's. What kind of choice was this? To lure the man she loved to his possible death, or to be the certain cause of her best friend's death? Despair gripped her, freezing her mind for an endless moment. "You don't want to kill Connie," she finally said, speaking softly so her friend wouldn't hear.

"No, you're right about that," Leroy said regretfully, shaking his head. "I'm planning on taking her with me, but plans can change." He stared at Gracie for a minute, then added, "It'll be your fault, you know. I don't want to hurt her, but if you won't cooperate . . ."

"She won't go."

"Sure she will. Connie and me have an understanding. Either she goes with me or that fiancé of hers will have himself a fatal accident." He looked over at Connie and said, "Isn't that right, sugar? You're going with me, aren't you?"

Connie didn't respond, didn't even move. Her

eyes had gone blank, glazed with fear and panic. Gracie wondered if she'd heard anything Leroy had said after his threat to kill Max and herself.

"What's it going to be, Sheriff?" Leroy asked, reaching out to stroke the gun barrel down her cheek. "Connie's pretty empty-headed, you know. I wonder what—"

"Dial the number," she said.

A distraction, that's what he needed, Max thought. Squinting through the crack in the tin shed, he had a surprisingly good view of Dunn holding a cell phone to Gracie's ear. He wished to hell he'd obeyed his instinct to hog-tie her so she couldn't go. Instead he'd let her walk right into this maniac's hands.

Every bit of the disaster was his fault. He'd screwed up the investigation from day one, when he'd looked into Grace O'Malley's big brown eyes and fallen for her like a ton of bricks. And if he didn't come up with a plan soon, Gracie would pay the ultimate price for his stupidity.

Dunn removed the phone from Gracie's ear and yelled at her. "Where is he? Tell me where he is."

"Asleep, probably," she said.

The deputy hit her, snapping her head back with the force of it. Max clenched his jaw and his fists against the need to go to her. But Dunn still had a gun, and he was far too close to Gracie for Max to risk it.

"You just don't know when to quit, do you?"

"I mean it," she said after a minute. "He's been sleeping a lot since the accident."

"He would've heard the phone."

"Not if he fell asleep on the couch."

Dunn cursed, ranting as he paced the room. Max had started toward the door to see if he could get a clear shot at him, when he heard a pickup driving over the rocky soil. He melted into the shadows. Old man Chapman climbed out, then reached back inside the truck and pulled out his shotgun. *Great*, Max thought. Now he had two of them to deal with.

Max put his eye to the crack again as Chapman threw open the door of the shed and leveled his gun at Dunn.

"What the hell are you doing here?" the deputy asked. "Put that gun down. Are you crazy?"

"Not anymore. But I sure must've been to let you talk me into this scheme in the first place."

Hallelujah, Max thought. Finally, a break. He crept toward the door and found a closer vantage point. The shed was ancient and riddled with cracks, making it easy to see inside. Chapman stood directly in the line of fire between himself and Dunn.

"Get out, old man. This is none of your concern."

"Be damned if it isn't, you scum-sucking lizard. I'm drawing the line, right here and now. Ain't no way I'll let you get away with murder."

"You're up to your ass in this, you fool. Better get out while you can. Besides, no one said anything about murder."

"I reckon you're just keeping that girl"—he gestured at Gracie—"here at gunpoint for fun, then." He glanced around, and the shotgun wavered. "What's Connie May doing here?" He lowered his arms and stared at Leroy. "You got no call to involve her. We made a deal. Reese isn't part of this."

" 'Reese isn't part of this,' " Dunn mimicked, and glanced toward the door, along the wall where Max couldn't see. "Connie May's going with me. I've been having her for months, and your son's too damned stupid to know it."

Chapman bellowed with rage and raised his gun to his shoulder. Dunn placed his pistol's gun barrel against Gracie's temple.

"Go ahead, old man. Shoot me."

Gracie's face had paled, but she didn't move. The next few seconds crawled by like an ice age and Max's heart stopped beating.

With shaking hands, Chapman lowered the shotgun. "What have I done?"

Dunn laughed and turned his pistol on Chapman. Max burst through the doorway, gun drawn and ready to shoot. Gracie swung her legs at the same moment, catching Dunn behind the knees and toppling him down in front of her.

Abandoning his shotgun, Chapman jumped into the fray. Max cursed, unable to risk a shot since he couldn't tell who was who in the tangled mess of people writhing on the floor. If he'd had just a moment longer, he'd have taken Dunn out, but Gracie couldn't have known that when she knocked him down. She'd reacted as he would have in the same situation, taking her only chance and hoping Chapman could help her.

Max started forward, hoping he could grab Dunn, or at least his pistol, then halted when Dunn shook Chapman off and came up with the gun himself. Raising to his knees, he aimed at Gracie. "You should've—"

Max shot him in the chest as the words left his mouth.

A look of pure shock came over his face. He dropped the gun, his hand going to his chest as he crumpled facedown.

Max reached Gracie first, more concerned with her than whether Dunn bled out or not. He pulled her into his arms and held her, unable to speak for the relief he felt.

"Boy, am I glad to see you," she said against his shoulder. "Things were getting downright dismal there for a minute."

The words were classic Gracie, but he heard the quiver in her voice. He released her and turned to see Chapman checking Dunn's pulse.

"Dead?"

"Not yet," Chapman said. "But he's bleedin' powerful bad."

Max took off his shirt and gave it to the old man. "Here, try to pack his wound and slow the bleeding."

"Max, do you think you could undo these handcuffs?" Gracie asked.

He found the keys attached to Dunn's belt. His hands were shaking as he freed her wrists and rubbed her shoulders to restore circulation. He heard her breath hiss in but she didn't speak. "Don't ever do anything like that again," he told her. "What did you think you were doing?"

She smiled at him. A beautiful sight, even with her split lip. "Stopping him from shooting Mr. Chapman, of course. I wasn't going to just sit there and watch him do it."

"Damn, Gracie, you could have been killed."

"Well, thanks to you, I wasn't."

He wanted to kiss her, but was afraid he'd hurt her mouth if he did, so he contented himself with hugging her again and kissing her hair and cheek.

"Connie," she said, pulling back. "We've got to untie her. Better call the ambulance and backup too."

"Reese isn't a part of this," Chapman said suddenly. "You know that, Gracie. You know Reese wouldn't—"

"Just what am I not a part of, Dad?"

Reese Chapman stood in the doorway of the tin shack, taking in the scene until his gaze fell on the woman still lying on the floor. "Oh, my God. Connie!" he cried, and rushed over to her.

"Give him my knife," Gracie said. "He'll never get those ropes off without it." She got to her feet, rubbing her arms and grimacing.

Max tossed Reese the knife. "Here, I'll take care of that now," he told the older man, and took over holding his shirt on Dunn's wound. Dunn's testimony was important to the case, but the vision of him holding Gracie at gunpoint still had Max by the throat. He didn't give a damn about the case right now. To his mind, dying was far too good for Dunn.

Gracie knelt beside him, touched Dunn's arm. "Leroy, the ambulance will be here soon."

His eyes fluttered open, and he stared at Gracie. With an effort he spoke. "Sorry."

"I know," she said softly. "I don't see a killer when I look at you."

FIFTEEN

Four days after the mess at the halfway house, as Gracie called it, life had almost settled back to normal. While she waited at the diner for Connie to sit down with her that afternoon, she thought over the way things had turned out.

With Leroy out of the loop, the big shipment of illegals never went through. Leroy gave up his contacts that same evening, and Border Patrol had picked them up before the culprits knew the ring had been broken. It came out, too, that the senior Chapman had been Border Patrol's anonymous tipster. That, along with his efforts to save Gracie, would play in his favor at his trial.

Gracie hoped he'd get off with probation. She couldn't face the thought of the old man in jail, even though allowing the smugglers to operate on his land had been wrong. The Chapman ranch had been one of the hardest hit when the cattle market bottomed out, and as she'd told Max, the problems with the EPA hadn't helped. Not to mention that she didn't doubt the smugglers had threatened violence to Chapman's family. Cooperating with them must have seemed like the only way out to the old man. Gracie had already forgiven him his part in it.

Leroy . . . Well, she had a much harder time forgiving him. First of all, he'd admitted to framing her father and that wasn't something she could readily forgive. He would do some serious prison time, though. When she thought about the lives he'd ruined and the misery he'd caused, all for greed, she couldn't drum up much sympathy for him. He might not be a murderer, but you sure as heck couldn't call him a good guy.

Max hadn't said a lot about Mr. Chapman, but he'd been loud and clear about what he thought Leroy deserved, she remembered with a smile. And now . . . Now his job was over. He'd accomplished what he set out to do—and a few things he hadn't intended, as well.

"You've got the saddest look on your face," Connie said, scooting into the booth seat across from her. "It's Max, isn't it? Is he still leaving?"

"Yep." She sipped her coffee and met Connie's concerned gaze. "This afternoon." She might look sad, Gracie thought, but she felt absolutely nothing when she said it. Numb, that was how she felt. Seemed like she ought to feel *something* when she knew for durn sure her heart was breaking.

Connie put her hand on Gracie's forearm and squeezed. "If Reese and I can try to work things out, there's no reason you and Max can't too."

Except that Max didn't believe they could. And she still didn't really understand why. "You know how glad I am about you and Reese, don't you?"

"It's hard to believe, isn't it? All this had made me realize how much I love him. The problem is—" Her voice cracked, and she started again. "He's forgiving me, but I'm having a hard time forgiving myself."

"You and Reese deserve to be happy."

"I hope we can be. Maybe with time, we'll work things out. But what are you going to do about Max?"

Gracie shrugged as though it didn't matter, but she knew she wasn't fooling her friend. "Nothing. He's made up his mind."

"Is that all you have to say?" Connie demanded incredulously. "You're just going to let him walk away without doing anything to stop him?"

Frustrated, she snapped back, "I don't have a whole heck of a lot of choice, do I? I can't force him to love me."

"No forcing about it." Connie waved a hand in disgust. "Any fool can see he's in love with you as much as you are with him. Don't tell me you haven't seen him looking at you like you're some dream he can't possibly have."

"I—I thought I'd imagined that. Figured it was wishful thinking."

"Girlfriend," Connie said, shaking her head, "that man is crazy about you."

"Right." Gracie glared at her. "If he's so crazy about me, then why is he leaving?"

"Have you tried to stop him? No, you've been mooning around doing nothing. I swear, Gracie, this isn't like you. Do something!"

"Like what? Arrest him?"

Connie grinned and cocked her head. "If that's what it takes, why not?"

Gracie stared at her for a moment, then her lips started to quiver. "No, don't tempt me. I can't do it."

"You're the sheriff. Sure you can."

"First I'm going to talk to him," Gracie said, rising and looking down at her friend.

"And if that doesn't work?"

"Then—" She slapped her hat on and flashed Connie a grin. "Then I'll handcuff him to the bed and have my way with him until he comes to his senses."

Since he hadn't brought much to begin with, it shouldn't have taken Max long to pack. He hadn't counted on memories slowing him down. His bag lay open on Gracie's bed, on top of the tangled mess of covers that gave testimony to how much of a hurry Gracie had been in when she finally left that morning. He closed his eyes and saw her face again, lost in passion, filled with love. Why did she have to be so damned sweet? he thought, his eyelids snapping open as he frowned. Why couldn't she have nagged him or lit into him for leaving, like any normal woman would have? Maybe then he wouldn't feel so guilty.

Picking up one of his faded blue work shirts, he remembered Gracie wearing it a few days earlier. Remembered what she'd looked like when he'd taken it off her too. He stuck it in his bag and reached for another shirt. Instead, his hand fell on the white T-shirt she'd slept in the night before. Part of the night, anyway. Hesitantly, his fingers closed on it. He picked it up and held it to his face. Her scent hit him like one of Jim Bob's gut punches, hard, fast, and breath stealing. Once he left, he'd never smell that scent again.

It shouldn't be so hard to leave her. The truth was, it wasn't hard. It was hell.

Dammit, he had to go! He tossed his shaving kit into his bag and zipped it part way shut. Didn't he?

Disgusted with himself, he paced to the window of her bedroom and stared outside. As usual during the heat of the day, the animals weren't very active. Caesar lay stretched out under the shade of an oak tree watching Boo, the three-legged hound dog, trying to scratch out a hole with his good leg. Slow going, Max thought, grinning, but Boo would get some help soon from one of the other dogs. One cat lay grooming itself beside Caesar, but most of the others had disappeared in search of cooler spots.

Gracie's rejects. The one thing they had in common was they all needed something from Gracie. And much as he didn't want to admit it, he needed her too. It scared him, that needing her. What if he accepted his need, accepted her love, and then something happened to her?

Was that what his problem was? Fear of loving her because he might lose her? He shoved his hands through his hair, glanced at his watch, and rubbed it while he thought about that. He'd become an emotional chicken, refusing to love because he was afraid of losing the person he loved. What he'd seen as a strength hadn't been strength at all. Only cowardice.

He couldn't visualize saying good-bye to Gracie. Couldn't imagine what it would be like never to see her smile at him again, or hear her laugh, or tell him she loved him. It made him ache just to think about leaving her. And when he thought about never making love with her again, he felt like banging his head against the window frame.

He turned away from the window, looking around the room. What if he stayed with her? Gracie had her own career, and a hell of a lot more independence than Marla had ever thought of having. She wouldn't have problems with his career; she was a cop herself.

His career. He didn't want to quit the Texas

Rangers. There was a simple way around that, though. He could transfer to the Ranger company that covered Bandido County. If he stayed, what would it be like?

"What the hell is that?" he asked aloud as the dogs outside started barking like crazy. Glancing out the window again, he saw a dark green pickup pulling away, throwing dust as it peeled out.

Curious, he ran through the hall to the living room, opened the front door, and stepped out onto the porch. A big, sad-eyed golden retriever sat beside a box full of . . . Puppies? Max squatted down beside the box. They were tumbling all over each other which made it hard to tell, but he thought he counted eight. Great, just what Gracie needed.

The other animals that had gathered around the box, lost interest fairly quickly and returned to lazing in the shade or digging holes underneath the porch, no doubt used to new additions to the club. Izzy, the spaniel mix who adored Max, sidled up to him and laid her head on his lap so he could pet her.

Hearing an engine, he wondered if the owners had changed their minds, but Gracie's patrol car ground to a halt in the driveway. A moment later she'd gotten out and was walking toward him with that slow, sure stride of hers, a smile and a pat for the animals surrounding her as she went. Sun glinted off her mirrored aviator sunglasses. A white hat shaded her face. She looked, he decided, almost exactly like she had the first time he saw her, right before she arrested him. The Sheriff from Hell, he thought, smiling.

"Surprise," he said. "Somebody just dumped them."

Gracie took off her glasses and stuck them in her shirt pocket before reaching down to pat the mother's head and scratch beneath her chin. "I know just how you feel, honey," she told the dog, her gaze lifting to meet Max's. "Or I will soon enough. Won't I?"

Damn, he felt like a jerk. Maybe because he was a jerk. And a fool to leave her. "Gracie—"

"How many are there?" she asked, not giving him a chance to fumble for an answer to an unanswerable question. Her hat came off, placed crown first on the porch swing. The gun belt followed. Sitting down next to him, she reached inside the box and pulled out a couple of the puppies, snuggling them against her chest.

"Eight. I think. Look, Gracie—"

"Aren't they cute?" she asked, holding up one reddish-blond fur ball and laughing as it licked her face. Several had escaped the box and were now tumbling over her lap and chewing on her khaki pants. The mother had snuggled up next to her and lay placidly wagging her tail. Not a one of them looked concerned, least of all Gracie.

Distracted for the moment, he asked, "What are you going to do with eight puppies and their mother?"

Watching one of the pups chase its tail, she smiled. "Feed them. Love them. Take care of them."

What she did for everyone, he mused, himself included. "The last thing you need is nine more animals. You've already got Noah's Ark."

Surprised, she glanced at him. "They won't be any trouble. Well, no more than the others, anyway. I'll find homes for the puppies. The mother shouldn't be too hard to place either, she's so pretty."

She cuddled one of the puppies in her arms and started laughing. "Look," she said, pointing at Max's leg.

One of the pups had latched on to the hem of his jeans and was tugging on it and growling. "You're a fierce one, aren't you?" Max picked it up. "Ouch," he said, as it promptly sank its sharp little teeth into his finger.

"I've got just the place for you," Gracie was telling the mother as she gathered the pups together and put them back in the box. "A nice, big stall that used to belong to a horse." She rose, picked up the box, and started for the barn. "Bring that puppy," she said to Max over her shoulder.

As he followed her, the pup wriggling underneath his arm, a realization struck Max like a two-by-four. Gracie didn't ration her love, she gave it away in massive doses to everyone who needed it. To Gracie love wasn't a burden, it was a joy.

"You amaze me," he said after they settled the mother and pups. "It doesn't even occur to you that you might regret taking on this responsibility."

She smiled at him. "How can you regret loving someone? The more love you give, the fuller your life is."

He took her face between his hands and looked into her eyes. "With all the love you have to give, your life ought to be filled to bursting."

"It could be," she whispered. "If you were in it."

She wanted him in her life. He wanted her to be in his. Wanted to wake up with her, love her, watch her grow big with his babies. Why had it taken him so long to see that he could have the love she offered? "Are you sure you know what you're getting into?"

"I'm sure. What about you?"

"I'm sure about one thing. I love you, Grace O'Malley. And I don't want to lose you." He set him mouth on hers and kissed her.

"About time you figured that out," she said when he let her up for air. "I thought I was going to have to throw you in jail to get you to realize it."

Laughing, he pulled her closer and nuzzled her neck. "So I'm a slow learner."

"I love you, Max," she said, wrapping her arms around his neck and hugging him.

"I know. I love you too. Even if it did take me

forever to admit it. Would you really have thrown me in jail?"

"Maybe." She nipped his lip. "I thought about handcuffs."

"Handcuffs?"

"Yep. I was going to cuff you to the bed."

"Sounds kinky," he said, and grinned. "I like that idea a lot better than jail. Tell me more." He kissed her again. "Better yet, show me more."

She did.

THE EDITORS' CORNER

Think about it. How would you react if love suddenly came up and bit you? Would you be ready to accept it into your life? Well, in the four LOVESWEPTs we have in store for you this month, each hero and heroine has to face those questions. Love takes them by surprise, and these characters, in true-to-life form, all deal with it in different fashions. We hope you enjoy reading how they handle that thing called love!

The ever-popular Fayrene Preston continues her Damaron Mark series with **THE DAMARON MARK: THE MAGIC MAN**, LOVESWEPT #878. Wyatt Damaron is sure he's dreaming. Even so, he can't resist following the lovely woman in period dress beckoning to him from the mist. As the mist recedes, Wyatt realizes that his sweet-talking sprite is flesh-and-blood contemporary Annie Logan. Wyatt is most definitely a man unlike any Annie has been used to, but something about the danger and passion lurking in his eyes has her thinking more than twice about him. He is a spellbinding sorcerer who promises to dazzle and amaze her, and in that he doesn't fail. He'd vowed to protect Annie from all that threatens to keep them apart, but will Annie trust him long enough to let him succeed? Fayrene doesn't disappoint in this sizzling novel that powerfully explores the fate of kindred spirits whose destinies are forever entwined.

Cheryln Biggs takes you on a high-speed chase through Louisiana low country in **HIDDEN TREASURE**, LOVESWEPT #879. Slade Morgan and Chelsea Reynolds are both out to recover a priceless pair of stolen antique perfume bottles—but for different reasons. For Slade it's a job he's been hired to do, for Chelsea it's a chance to prove she can accomplish more for her company in the field than behind a desk. A dangerous game of cat and mouse ensues, making for close quarters and breathless adventure. You'll be glad you came along for the ride as one reckless rebel of a hero meets his match in an unlikely damsel in distress.

Author Catherine Mulvany returns at her humorous best with her second LOVESWEPT, #880. Mallory Scott has always had trouble trusting men. Wouldn't you be **MAN SHY** if your boyfriend of eleven years left you for your own sister? Now Mallory has to find a date for the happy couple's upcoming nuptials. But he can't be just any man, he has to be one hunk of a guy. Enter Brody Hunter. Sexy mouth, silver gray eyes, tousled chocolate brown hair—in short, drop-dead gorgeous. More than enough man to ward off the pitying looks sure to be given her at the wedding. Brody can't understand why the beautiful Mallory has to hunt for an escort, but who is he to argue with good fortune? Will the potent attraction they feel be strong enough to convince Mallory to drop the carefully planned game of let's pretend? Let Catherine Mulvany show you in this outrageous romp of a romance!

Please welcome newcomer Caragh O'Brien and her stunningly sensual debut, **MASTER TOUCH**, LOVESWEPT #881. When worldly art dealer Milo Dansforth requests art restorer Therese Carroll's services, she's not sure she wants the hassle. She's quite satisfied with her quiet existence. But Milo is counting on Therese's loyalty to her father to ensure that she'll take on the job—she's the only one with the expertise to do the restoration on his priceless portrait. In a makeshift art conservatory set up in a Boston studio, Therese races the clock to finish the project and discover the secrets that lay beneath the surface of both the painting and its mysterious owner. Milo tantalizes Therese with his every touch, and suddenly the painting is not the only thing these two lovers have in common. Caragh O'Brien's talent shines bright in this tapestry of tender emotion and breath-stealing mystique. Look for more from Caragh in the near future!

Happy reading!

With warmest wishes,

Susann Brailey

Joy Abella

Susann Brailey
Senior Editor

Joy Abella
Administrative Editor